Rum Raisin Rendezvous

Harriet G. Fry

First Published in 2022 by Blossom Spring Publishing
Rum Raisin Rendezvous
Copyright © 2022 Harriet G. Fry
ISBN 978-1-7397357-0-8
E: admin@blossomspringpublishing.com
W: www.blossomspringpublishing.com
Published in the United Kingdom. All rights reserved

To Jessica

Chapter 1

It's no secret that yours truly, Mattie Bryant, wanted out of the classroom. I came to this realization after less than three years on the job. The whole teaching scene wasn't on my radar. Marriage to Peter Dawson was. Once that happened, I figured I'd have more time to find out exactly what kind of a career I might merge with that of being Mrs. Peter Dawson.

Word to the wise: Don't expect to find out what makes you tick by planning to tie the knot with someone who's scared of knots!

On Thanksgiving Day, Peter had graced my ring finger with a lovely diamond.

"Mattie will choose our wedding date!" Peter announced to our friends gathered round the holiday table. I was over the moon.

I wanted a "school's-out" wedding—who wanted to worry about writing lesson plans and grading papers plans right after coming back from a romantic honeymoon!

"Let's do it on the first of July!" I suggested and, happily, Peter agreed. For forty-eight hours, that is. No sooner did the long Thanksgiving weekend come to a close than Peter began pushing back. *Who* did he say would choose our wedding date?

Before the year was out, Peter changed his mind three times*: Let's move the month back from July to September, Mathilde. It will be cooler.* (We live in Florida! It's warm year round!) Then it was, *Mathilde, how about us moving our big day from September to November? It'll be symbolic to get hitched during the same month we got engaged.* (Excuse me? That's so high school!) Finally, going full circle Peter decided that July would be great for our nuptials after all. Then he threw a curve.

"Not *next* July, Mathilde. I mean July of the *following* year. We'll have more time!"

"More time for what?" I asked.

My question hung in the air. It's still hanging there. Enough said.

I should have realized that Peter had cold feet when he shifted from my preferred *Mattie* to my oh-so-formal-sounding given name every time the wedding date debate came up. As January moved along, Peter and I were not getting any warmer or cozier where firming up a wedding date was concerned. By April I decided enough was enough.

After a wordless lunch at my place one Sunday afternoon, I took off my diamond and handed it to Peter before he could get comfortable with the remote. I never in my life saw anyone so visibly relieved to receive a piece of jewelry.

"I think breaking our engagement works, Mathilde. You're not ready yet."

Who's not ready? I held my tongue. I guess he read my mind. He stuck the ring in his pocket, handed me the remote, picked up his jacket and was gone with the wind.

I could live with that. What I couldn't live with was going back to work Monday with a naked ring finger. It was bad enough having to go to job I disliked. It was worse at lunch period, showing up in the teachers' lounge only to be subjected to so many sympathetic glances you'd have thought somebody died. The end of the academic year couldn't come fast enough. And then, Ig-Loo fell in my lap.

After many years on Biscayne Bay, my dad's brother Igor—Uncle Ig to us nieces and nephews—and his wife Louise—she preferred being *Loo* "for professional reasons"—decided to retire. Unfortunately, their namesake, Ig—Loo, a little ice cream shop at Miami's Bayside Market, hadn't attracted a single serious buyer.

"Just lookers, the ones who say, 'I'll think about it' then we never hear from them again," Uncle Ig lamented when I stopped by Ig—Loo for a cool cone on a hot Miami afternoon. The For Sale sign was still posted over Ig—Loo's entrance. Aunt Louise was especially unhappy with the lack of prospective buyers. She was as anxious as Uncle Igor to start a new chapter in their lives. Their plan—a bucket list dream——was to travel the USA together in a brand new RV. Uncle Ig had just purchased one and had christened it *Born To Roam*. The two were anxious to start their adventure of a lifetime in their brand new home on wheels.

"But we won't leave until we know Ig—Loo is in good hands," my aunt insisted. "Ideally, we want to get acquainted with the people who eventually take over this place."

"It would be great if someone in the family were interested," my uncle added as he scooped me a double Strawberry in a waffle cone. He and my aunt exchanged a glance.

Uncle Ig winked as he handed me my cone. "On the house as always for you, Mattie," he said.

"In more ways than one," Aunt Loo added. She looked me square in the eyes as if she were trying to read my mind. But I wasn't thinking about anything in particular. I was too engrossed in polishing off my ice cream. It had to be almost one hundred degrees outdoors. The cool, smooth ice cream and plump strawberries hit the spot!

Uncle Ig came around the counter. "We know you want to leave your job," he said. "Your folks told us you've had it with teaching."

"And then that mess with Peter last year...." my aunt chimed in.

Uncle Ig nodded. "You're okay being done with that stick—in—the—mud Dawson fellow, aren't you, Mattie?"

Hmmm, I thought, these two are psyching me out for some reason. I dabbed my lips with a napkin.

"To your and Aunt Loo's questions and concerns, yes and yes," I assured my uncle.

I hoped I was convincing. While I was truthful about needing a career change, I didn't know if I was better off for breaking up with Peter Dawson. Some days I felt liberated, like I wasn't in an emotional limbo anymore. Still, other days, I missed the "old days" with

Peter. We'd had fun times dating during college, where we'd met, and then afterwards when we fell in love, we naturally assumed we'd eventually get married. I was establishing a teaching career—or so I thought that's what I thought doing, never dreaming I wouldn't like the profession as much as I'd imagined I would—and Peter was in his element in Miami's thriving economy as sales director for a luxury class automobile dealership. We had it all. When he proposed, I accepted in a heartbeat. The diamond engagement ring he presented me was gorgeous, a Teardrop, my favorite cutting.

Then it all changed suddenly and, at least as I saw it, permanently. Peter wasn't the outgoing, confident guy I'd fallen for, and even decided to leave the job he'd so enjoyed to start driving for a taxi service. *It's easier driving cars than selling them, Mathilde.*

It was almost as though he wanted to scare me into thinking the time really wasn't right for us to wed, that his job didn't pay enough. Sure enough, one day he actually said so. Was the love of my life so afraid of commitment that he'd interrupt his career to take a low paying job just so he could lean on another excuse to put off a marriage that I believed he wanted as much as I did?

After a year and a half of waiting for my beautiful teardrop diamond to have a band of gold for company, I'd decided it was time to part company with that waiting game, and with Peter.

The scent of Aunt Loo's signature floral bouquet cologne brought me back to the moment. She leaned in close to my ear.

"What we're saying Mattie, is that Ig—Loo is yours if you want it," she whispered.

I was sure I heard wrong. I spun around.

"You want me to buy Ig—Loo?" I asked through a mouthful of waffle and strawberry.

"Yes, we do," Uncle Ig smiled and handed me another napkin. "You missed a spot, right there," he said, pointing to my chin.

"Now, don't worry about money," Aunt Loo

went on. "We'll sell Ig—Loo to you for one dollar. What do you say, Mattie? Your uncle and I can't think of a more trustworthy person to take over our Ig—Loo...rather, *your* Ig—Loo, if you want it..."

"We're downsizing to that RV," Uncle Ig explained. We don't need more stuff. We kept what we wanted of our sentimental things when we sold the house."

Whoa! This was news. "You *sold* your house?"

I couldn't imagine my aunt and uncle leaving their neighborhood in Wynwood Art District. Establishing Ig—Loo on the Bayfront, south of Wynwood, was as far as my uncle and aunt had been willing to travel without leaving Miami—Dade. Greater Miami was their home. They never even vacationed out of town.

Uncle Ig leaped right over my question. "Just look at how many people come down *here,* for *their* vacations! They know a good endless summer getaway when they see it. But we *lived it!* Now it's time for Loo and me to do a different kind living ourselves! We want to go on a... "

Aunt Loo jumped in, "Not *want* to, we're *going*! Your uncle and I are taking a cross—country adventure. It's time to have some fun, right Ig?"

Uncle Ig nodded. "You bet!" He turned to me again. "What do you say, Mattie? Want to be a hard-working business owner instead of a burnt out school teacher?"

Putting it *that* way, how could I decline? This was it, an opportunity to start a new career, right here by Miami's beautiful Biscayne Bay. Miami was my hometown. While I'd thought of making a new start somewhere else, I never really wanted to leave Miami. And right here, at the Bayside Marketplace, I now had a golden opportunity to become a business owner of Ig—Loo, one of the most popular shops along the Bayfront. I'd be known as *Mattie Bryant, Proprietor.* Just the thought gave me goosebumps! It sure sounded better than

*Miss   Mathilde,   Tired   Teacher—Bride—In—
Waiting*...and waiting...and waiting...

Chapter 2

Jo and Bea have an idea they want to run by me. Hey, I'm all ears. It's been two months since I took ownership of Ig—Loo. I can't believe how fast the time has passed. It seems like just the other day I accompanied my aunt and uncle to the law firm that handled all the dotting of the i's and crossing of the t's required to transfer a business, and all the checks and balances that went with it. There were documents galore to read, sign, witness, stamp and seal. *To close a one—dollar sale,* I thought, *it sure takes a lot of work!*

I'm glad I said yes when Uncle Ig asked me if I wanted to keep Ig—Loo's full time counter ladies, Joanne Blake and Bea Martin, onboard. If I thought there was a lot of behind the scenes paper shuffling to go through just to make Ig—Loo officially mine, I was floored by how much work behind the ice cream display freezer went into keeping Ig—Loo operating in the black! My uncle and aunt had made good profits running Ig—Loo with a business model that proved tried and true: great customer service, a specialized menu that offered only the six most traditional flavors—chocolate, butter almond, vanilla, strawberry, chocolate—chip mint, and coffee——and doing all their bookkeeping themselves by hand up until just before they retired. Bea, who was very good with a computer, had updated the ledgers shortly before Ig—Loo changed hands.

"When Igor and Loo put Ig—Loo on the market, they figured it would be better to have a more streamlined bookkeeping system." Bea explained. We were talking shop from behind the counter as we waited for customers one afternoon. Like most of the past few weeks, customer traffic that day had been on the slow side.

"I offered to update how we kept the books," Bea went on. "Igor was astonished by how fast those receipts could be compiled on a single spreadsheet and printed. Your aunt was so impressed she wanted to learn the app, too!" We both smiled at the idea of Aunt Loo using a computer. She did great, though, Bea said. And so did Jo, even though Joanne's favorite job was working the cash register. Ig—Loo still kept the old mechanical kind.

"Maybe we'll go digital with the cash register," I suggested.

Bea laughed. "It would have to be with Jo's blessing. She loves pulling the lever on that old machine and hearing the bell ring."

We agreed that the new digital bookkeeping system was easier, to keep us up with the times. And while Joanne loved the old reliable cash register that Uncle Igor started out with all those years ago, Bea said that Jo thought Ig—Loo could use a product *and* publicity facelift.

"New owner, new image, was how she put it." Bea peered out the window at the tourists taking selfies and strolling along the Bayfront promenade.

"And that's where your idea comes in?" I

asked Bea. She nodded.

"Have you heard of a place called The Tasty Glacier? It's a new ice cream parlor in Coconut Grove."

I had not. But I was about to, thanks to Elfie.

...

"You want one scoop of Double—R?"

What's that, a ranch in West Texas?" I joked. The teenager rolled her eyes.

"Duh...give me a break," she droned.

"I'm sorry, honey. I was just kidding," I said. I couldn't take my eyes off her outfit. Her bright red sundress was adorned with tiny round jingle bells and miniature plastic fruits. Atop her head she wore a fantasizer heaped with poufs of glittered purple and white tulle. Nestled in the center of the nest of tulle...was a little doll that resembled, of all things, an elf.

It had been the longest, most boring day, with only a handful of customers, until this gal showed up. As weird as she looked in that wild costume she was wearing, I made an effort to provide the all—important customer service. I listened attentively as she interpreted, evidently for my benefit. After all, I wasn't young and hip, and she essentially told me so!

"*All* the kids know that Double R means *Rum Raisin...*"

"I'm a twentysomething," I said. "When I was your age, we didn't give nicknames to ice cream flavors."

"What's my age?" she asked with a shrug. *How snarky can you get?* I thought as I continued to scrutinize her outfit in spite of myself.

The girl kept talking. "The Tasty Glacier down in The Grove has Double—R. It's awesome. Do you sell it?" She waved a slender, henna art—embellished arm over her head and twirled a few times before the three of us. Jo stood there open—mouthed, dumbstruck. Bea was suppressing a giggle. I was happy to have some entertainment to break up the monotony of waiting for some brisk business. Still, there was something about this girl that rubbed me the wrong way.

"I also make doll—friend fascinators," she continued, tapping her fascinator with her long, glossy hot pink colored finger nails. The little elf figurine bobbed up and down as her finger tips made contact with the layers of tulle. Her sundress swayed to her movement and the strings of bells jingle—jangled around the plastic fruits.

Good grief, what had I been missing during my years teaching elementary school? Is this what the high schoolers were wearing nowadays?

"Well, do you or don't you have Double R?" the girl asked.

I'd lost focus. All that bling, I thought. And she was actually selling it. I wished Ig—Loo had a gimmick like that to boost foot traffic.

"We do, I, I mean, we *don't*, unfortunately, right now," I stammered. "But we will," I added quickly. The last thing I wanted was to admit to our customers that we didn't stock something they wanted, even if they were weird dressers with attitude.

I pointed to the chalkboard menu hanging on the wall behind me.

"Right now, we are still offering Ig—Loo's traditional flavors. They're all delicious. Would you like to sample a spoonful of something?"

Before the girl could answer, Bea was practically climbing over the freezer.

"Why Miss, I absolutely love what you're wearing!" she gushed. "Is that a 'lil doll or something, peeking out of the top up there? Oh. My. Goodness. It *is*! It's an *elf*!"

The girl beamed. "You know about fascinators?"

"I sure do," Bea said. "Yours is very unique. In my day, why, if we wanted to jazz up our hair styles, we just tied on a ribbon, maybe add a barrette or two. You have a real work of art there, my dear!"

"Yes, I do, thank you," the girl said, breaking into a smile. "I'm so glad you like it."

I watched Bea work her charm on this testy young customer, wishing I could pour it on like that! *Work of art?* But hey, the customer's always right, right? Bea then apologized for Ig—Loo being *temporarily* out of Double R.

"We're under new management," she explained, adding, "and we're in the process of expanding our flavors menu."

Are we, Bea? We're thinking, planning. We haven't actually moved on anything yet!

The girl seemed to soften. She smiled at the three of us and turned her attention to Ig—Loo's limited menu. She seemed to take forever deciding. I held my tongue as I felt my patience wane. *It won't take long to read through it, honey! Come on, already! Pick one of our standards or go back to that new place, the tasty whatever!*

"The butter almond's especially yummy." Bea suggested, steering the girl. "You and your little friend up there in your hair will love it, I promise. And it's our treat, how about that?"

Bea's approach worked. The girl gave in,

happily accepting a cone of butter almond on the house. She took a lick and gave a thumbs—up.

"It's not a Double—R," she said, "But it's delish, thank you!"

Bea beamed. "Come see us again, Miss!"

"Call me Elfie!" the girl called back, as she headed out into Miami's late afternoon Bayside shoppers.

Maybe the girl and her little elf doo—dad had brought us some luck. Maybe she'd pointed out Ig—Loo to a few tourists who might have noticed her ice cream—possibly after first noticing her head gear and background music!——and asked where to buy some. Who knows how it happened, but for the rest of the day, Ig—Loo hopped like old times. Everybody and their fifth cousins, it seemed, walked through Ig—Loo's door. We stayed open later than usual, enjoying the crowd (and the *cha—ching* of Jo's cash register!), finally closing up well past the dinner hour.

"I don't know about you two," Jo said, "but I'm too tired to cook tonight!"

"Me, too," Bea said. Want to grab some supper before we go home?"

I had other things on my mind. Maybe in the sudden rush of business, Jo and Bea had forgotten that they had something to tell me that had to do with that new ice cream parlor, The Tasty Glacier. I didn't forget, though. Nor would I forget Elfie, and how she had wandered into Ig—Loo specifically asking for an ice cream flavor she'd discovered there.

Bea nudged me with a plump elbow. "Wake up, Mattie! I'm in the mood for pizza. So is Joanne. Want to come with us?"

My stomach was growling. But my curiosity about the Tasty Glacier won out.

"No thanks, Bea. You and Jo go on without me. I'm heading home. See you tomorrow."

I didn't lie. I *did* head home, to change out of my bright blue Ig—Loo tee shirt and slacks and into something drab. Then I drove to Coconut Grove. It was time to gather some intelligence at The Tasty Glacier.

Chapter 3

"We're here!" Joanne called from the patio.

I hurried to the sliding door to help Jo and Bea in with their parcels. After my secret mission last evening to Coconut Grove, I placed calls to both ladies and asked them to come by my place this morning for breakfast before we opened Ig—Loo for the day. Bea offered to bring some homemade blueberry muffins to go with my eggs and cheese scramble. Jo toted a container of what looked like fresh squeezed orange juice. She opened the container and invited me to take a sniff. There was more than orange juice going on in there!

"It's slightly, shall I say, *compromised*," she said, winking, as we set the table. "You're telling me!' I remarked. I was really surprised that Jo would want a cocktail at 8 o'clock in the morning.

Joanne poured Bea and me a sampling of

her citrus concoction. "We have here a mixture of pineapple juice, ginger, and sparkling Sangria," she said, doing a goblet stir.

Bea sniffed the concoction. "Why include the Sangria?"

"Don't you *remember*, Bea?" Jo raised an eyebrow.

"Oh, that's right!" Bea squealed, biting her lip. Her cheeks flushed bright pink. I was sure this was an inside joke, and Bea had unwittingly exposed the tip of the punch line. I decided to play along and not press for an explanation. Besides, I had my recon briefing to report, *if* I could just get Jo and Bea to settle in.

I held up my wine goblet. "Moving right along…"

Bea got the message. "A toast, then!" she announced, recovering from her faux pas and raising her glass. Joanne joined in.

"To Ig—Loo!" she cheered. We clinked goblets and kicked back.

Jo's concoction was absolutely delicious,

even for the early hour!

Between Jo's yummy beverage, my never—fail eggs—and—cheese scramble, and Bea's outstanding blueberry muffins to go with some fresh brewed coffee, we ate well and talked up a storm about everything from Bea's daughter's upcoming graduation from nursing school to Jo's newest addition to her menagerie of pets, a rescue mutt named Hi—ya who, Jo said, adored cold, leftover pizza.

"Speaking of pizza, how was supper last night? I asked.

"Not as delish as what we've got right here at this table, but Hi—ya liked her doggie bag just fine, " Jo said.

Bea turned to me. "Did you make time to eat last night, or did you just come back here and crash?"

I checked my watch and dodged Bea's question. "C'mon, gals," I urged. "Give me your big idea before we get a breakfast buzz! We have to open Ig—Loo soon!"

Playing dumb was getting hard, I admit. I

wanted to blurt out where I'd gone the previous evening, but I wanted to hear what Bea and Jo had up their sleeves first.

Bea turned to Jo. "I think you should tell Mattie, Joanne. After all, *you* spiked the juice."

"Right." Jo stood up as though she were making a presentation to a room of suits on some board of directors.

"Bea and I think Ig—Loo needs to expand its menu to include snazzier, jazzier flavors. That's why I spiked the oh—jay this morning. It was my lead in, to preview what our menu could convey." Jo let out a hiccup as she lowered herself into her chair.

"Sorry, it must be the alcohol!" she giggled.

I didn't like where this was going. One minute she was all business, and the next she was acting like she'd just wrapped up Happy Hour.

"Jo, we can't sell alcohol—laced ice cream, especially to the kids!"

Bea jumped in. "Jo doesn't mean we should spike our ice cream, Mattie! Look how exciting, how much fun, our breakfast became this morning just by introducing something new. No pun intended here, Mattie, but we really do need to spike our menu. Do that, and we've spiked our profit margin, too!"

Jo tossed her formal presentation. She stood up again and began prancing around my kitchen like, well, like a kid in an ice cream shop!

"Remember yesterday, Mattie? Remember the customer, Elfie, she called herself, with all of the bells on her clothes and that fascinator on her head?"

I squeezed my eyes shut and grinned at the memory of a slow morning suddenly breaking Ig—Loo's record—at least since I'd taken the helm——for ice cream sales in a single day. Elfie had to have brought us luck, I believed, and I voiced as much at our pow—wow.

"I doubt any of us can forget Elfie, Jo. I'm convinced she brought more foot traffic to us yesterday just by walking through Bayside Marketplace in her one—of—a—kind outfit."

Bea chimed in. "But what's more, did you notice how, when she walked into Ig—Loo, she expected to get exactly what she wanted, and how surprised she was to learn we didn't even know what a Double R was, let alone have it on our menu? She must be able to pick up on what's trending around town a heck of lot better than we can."

"Oh, I wouldn't say that," I said. It was time to drop the bomb. "In fact, I found out about what's happening in Coconut Grove...."

My tease went right over Jo's head. Bea's too. Those two were on a roll.

"That kid can give a lot of publicity to Ig—Loo, too," Jo was saying.

"Imagine what she could do *outside* Ig—Loo, as a greeter!" Bea exclaimed. "Elfie could give out free samples of our newest flavors...when we *get* new flavors, that is!"

Giving free samples seemed like a good idea. But hiring Elfie to greet passersby was another thing. Would she even be willing to wear the Ig—Loo uniform? I'd kept up the original Ig—

Loo dress code that my uncle and aunt had chosen from the start: bright blue visors with matching tees, and white slacks or skirts. Our clothes wouldn't play jingle bells music while we scooped ice cream, and we wouldn't cozy up to wearing plastic figurines atop the brims of our visors.

As for coming up with a wider menu for Ig—Loo, my recon mission to The Tasty Glacier was the mother of all wake—up calls. Ig—Loo had to at least match, if not exceed, the variety of offerings available at Tasty Glacier.

I turned to Jo. "Does rum raisin ice cream *have* to contain real rum?"

Jo shrugged. "I don't know. But whatever the flavor, if we spiked it, we'd have to obtain a liquor license to serve and sell, right? And we'd have to card our customers, especially minors who are trying to look older. Do we want to jump through all those hoops?"

Jo was right about that. I didn't want to check everyone's age just to sell ice cream. Tasty Glacier's Double R rum flavored ice cream really was out of this world. Whether that rum flavor came from the real thing, or an extract, it was impossible to tell.

"Okay, let's add rum raisin to our menu, but without the alcohol," I announced then and there.

"If our supplier can get it for us," Bea said.

Bea had a point. Ig—Loo's ice cream came to us already manufactured, from a very reputable wholesale distributer, and at a very fair price. I wanted to keep it that way. Would I be able to, or did the public prefer their ice cream 'homemade', 'organic', 'lactose—free' or, heaven help us 'designer' these days?

"Makes you kind of tempted to just go along with Ig—Loo's six traditional flavors and forget the whole modernization thing," Jo mused.

I was damned if I'd end up sounding like Peter Dawson, all undecided and scared of my own shadow!

"No deal, Jo, we either move forward or we're done."

"Or we're *done*?" Bea echoed.

I couldn't keep quiet any longer. "The Tasty Glacier was buzzing last night," I blurted.

"We know, Mattie," Bea said.

I thought I'd heard wrong. "What? You *know*?"

Bea reached into her tote bag. "We found this outside. It was lying on your welcome mat." She handed me a slip of paper. My receipt for the cone of Double R! It must have fallen out of my bag while I was fishing for my house key. Jo brought her specs down to the tip of her freckled nose and raised her eyebrows as she peered over the rims.

"Ah *HA!* So *that's* where you went after work yesterday! You chose a Double R at The Tasty Glacier over a pizza supper with Bea and me! You went spying, did you not?"

"I cannot tell a lie," I lied. As I saw it, it wasn't spying. It was *observing, unnoticed*. And I told Jo so. She didn't buy it. Neither did Bea.

"Cut the semantics, Mattie!" she boomed, crossing her arms over her chest. "Tell us *everything*!" The twinkle in her eye belied her serious side. Bea was as excited to get a briefing about The Tasty Glacier as I was to give one. Still....

I ripped up the receipt, balled the paper shreds and aimed for a clean shot into the wastepaper basket.

Jo leaned in. "Destroying the evidence, Mattie?" Who else should, or should not, know that you went to Coconut Grove last night? What's with all the cloak—and—dagger?"

I knew I'd eventually have to explain to Bea and Jo how it bothered me that my little shop was lacking. It irked me no end that my aunt and uncle had enjoyed such success with Ig— Loo for such a long time, by keeping things simple. Why hadn't it worked that well for me so far? We'd had strings of days so slow that oftentimes I felt like Ig—Loo was a seasonal operation. Nothing could be further from the truth.

"Ladies, I didn't tell you what I was up to last night because I was afraid you'd either try to stop me or try to follow me. Do you want to know what I saw over there?"

"Does my new mutt love cold pizza?" Jo chuckled.

I glanced at the kitchen clock. We were really running late now. "Let's go, we'll talk more on the way to work."

By the time we arrived at Ig—Loo, Bea and Jo had a mental picture of what I'd seen firsthand at The Tasty Glacier. I told them how enormous the place was compared to Ig—Loo, how many more flavors it carried, and as many catchy names as I could remember, all written in confetti colors in paperless format: a huge menu digitally imposed on a floor—to—ceiling whiteboard framed with ice blue neon tube lighting boasted a mouthwatering ice cream flavors with creative names like *Blackberry Bonanza, Licorice Ribbon, Triple Tangerine, Whaz—A—Matta—Marshmallow, Choco— Iceberg, and of course, the Double R.* I had, in our short walk from my house to Bayside Marketplace, also packed in a detailed description of the glacier—themed décor.

"Tasty Glacier has silvery wind chimes shaped like icicles hanging from the ceiling, dozens of them. All the walls are iridescent light blue, just like icebergs!" I told Jo and Bea how I'd felt like I was in an Arctic ice cave, right in the middle of balmy Coconut Grove.

Jo smiled as I unlocked the door to Ig—Loo and flipped the OPEN sign on the door.

"You beat us to it, Mattie," she said. "Bea and I had thought of doing a little snooping over there ourselves. Well, now we know. Tasty Glacier sounds like quite an operation. It's so much more than the Double R. It's an *experience.*"

"Exactly! And we've got make coming to Ig— Loo just as much of a destination spot, even if it has to be on a smaller scale. There's no excuse for our having slow days. This is Miami! We're on the Bayfront! People are everywhere. Ig—Loo is not going to be ho— hummed out of the competition. We're not the so—called poor relation to Tasty Glacier!"

If I was sounding hard—nosed, it was because I was scared. Ig—Loo had to start turning a consistent profit. The idea of returning to the classroom was not an option any more than planning a life with Peter had been. Some bridges, I discovered, have to burn so that there's nothing else to do but take a leap of faith. Taking the reins of Ig—Loo was one of those leaps I had to make good on. There was no turning back.

As we readied Ig—Loo for the day's business, I remembered another detail that had turned my head the night before.

"The Tasty Glacier accepts Bitcoin!"

Bea looked at Jo.

"Huh?"

Jo looked at me.

"What is that?"

Oh, no, I thought, *better not move so fast!*

Chapter 4

Bea was waiting for me outside Ig-loo, pacing back and forth. Even from a distance, I could see she was flustered. A heavier than usual summer rainstorm had rolled in overnight and I prayed Ig—Loo hadn't fallen victim to water damage.

"Don't come in," Bea said as I approached. Oh no, I thought. It's bad.

"I have to see for myself, Bea. If there's water damage from the storm, I have to make some calls to the insurance company, and the plumber, as well as..."

"No, no. It's not that," Bea interrupted, shaking her head. She pointed to Ig—Loo's front door.

"*Peter's* here, Mattie."

Bea didn't have to say another word. Goosebumps galore raced up my arm like ants. It was bad inside my little ice cream shop, all right, just not the kind of bad I'd anticipated.

I'm leaving, I silently mouthed to Bea and turned on my heels.

At the Bayside Marketplace promenade, I got lost in the late morning throng of tourists, shoppers, ferryboat tour lines and souvenirs kiosks. If I looked out of place in my Ig—Loo uniform, nobody seemed to notice.

My heart was racing, though not faster than my thoughts. Why was I so afraid to see Peter again? I didn't hate him. He didn't hate me. We'd known each other since our college years. Maybe we weren't each other's best mate—match, but wasn't there anything salvageable from our having been together for 4 years?

I left the ferry boat dock and walked back through the Marketplace to Ig—Loo. The goosebumps were gone, but I gave myself a mini pep talk just the same. *Mattie, you have more bounce—back potential than you think you do. You have a whole new career, a whole new direction. There's nothing scary about selling a cone of ice cream to your ex—fiancé. For that matter, maybe you should give him a cone for free to promote Ig—Loo! Hadn't Bea done just that with Elfie?*

Then it hit me: *Wait a minute, Mattie. Peter Dawson never touches ice cream.*

How could I have forgotten? *Useless calories*, was how Peter defined what many folks considered the best course of any meal: the dessert! Once, I'd told Peter he sounded like a weight loss commercial. He had taken that as a compliment, believe it or not!

So, what would my ex—fiancé be doing in Ig—Loo? Except, maybe, looking for me? Bring it on, then!

I walked into Ig—Loo like I owned the place. Shoot, I *did* own it! And nobody was going frighten me away, no matter what.

...

"Geez, Mattie, even Jo isn't that short sighted, even with her glasses off!"

Bea laughed as she cut second helping slices of pie for Jo and me. After the dreadful screw—up at Ig—Loo, we needed to turn lemons into lemon meringue. We were closing out our day at Bea's condo, indulging in another of her memorial homemade goodies. Though I'd put on a few pounds since opening Ig—Loo, I was determined to satisfy my need to forget about what had happened after I walked back into my little ice cream shop, determined not to let Peter's unexpected presence get the best of me.

I gave Bea a thumbs—up as I dug into the fluffy meringue and silky lemon curd. "You missed your calling, Bea! You should have opened your own bakery!"

"Glad you like!" Bea beamed.

Peter would have admonished Bea's rich baked goods as useless calories and a bad influence on good nutrition, just as he shunned ice cream. As Jo and I saw it, though, there was absolutely nothing "useless" about anything Bea took out of her oven. It was *all* good!

At Bea's table, I almost reflected aloud on Peter's opinion of all things *dolce* but I held my tongue. It wouldn't have helped to bring him up in conversation right now, especially after what had happened at Ig—Loo this morning. The whole mess was still fresh in our minds, which was why Bea's comfort food was so necessary! We needed to laugh the major mix—up away, any way we could.

When I returned to Ig—Loo from my temporary hi—tail, only one customer was at the counter waiting for Jo to ring up his purchases. From behind, he was Peter all right. Tall and slim, and carrying a buckskin satchel that looked just like the one I'd given him on his birthday before the year before our engagement. I was surprised he was still using it, considering I'd given him back his ring long ago.

I gathered my wits, pulled up behind him and, summoning my brightest smile—that was hard!——tapped his shoulder.

"Hi, Peter, remember me?"

The man who turned and returned my smile was not Peter.

My own smile faded fast. I stepped back, practically tripping over myself

"I am *so* sorry, sir. I thought you were someone I hadn't seen in a long time."

"Well, lucky him," the stranger replied. Unlike me, his smile remained. It was a beautiful one, spread beneath a neatly trimmed mustache. Another thing Peter wouldn't consider trying, along with high— calories desserts.

"I wish someone would remember *me* with such enthusiasm," he added. His British accent was charming.

I became giddy and embarrassed at the same time. Fortunately, Jo saved the day.

"I'm Joanne," she extended her hand across the register. "And this is Mattie, the owner of Ig—Loo. We also have Bea. Where'd she go?" Jo craned her neck for signs of Bea.

"I guess she's on her break," I offered. I had a suspicion, though, that Bea may have realized that she had not seen Peter after all and was in hiding.

"Pleased to meet you both, I'm Carl Statler." We shook hands all around. His grasp was strong and assured, his deep blue eyes penetrating, drawing me in. Carl Statler wasn't just gorgeous, he was an Englishman! Some women I know perk up when they see a man in uniform, but I'm more the foreign accent type. If Peter had had one, who knows? I may have kept that ring on my finger a little longer...

"Are you touring Bayside today, Mister Statler?" Jo asked.

"Yes and no," Carl answered, still looking at me before catching is manners and turning his attention to Jo. I have to admit, I was immediately annoyed by his shift of focus. Nobody had looked at me with such interest in a long time.

"I live in Gainesville." He flashed his college class ring. It was the only ring on his left hand.

Jo leaned in to scrutinize the ring. "Ah! The University of Florida! You're an alum, Mister Statler?"

Carl laughed. "I am, and a diehard Gators fan. And ladies, please call me Carl."

Jo was beside herself. "I adore basketball! I follow all the teams!"

Did I mention that, besides saving homeless animals, she's a basketball groupie?

"The game amazes me, no matter who's playing," she added.

"Well, we have to have a proper chat about the sport one of these days," Carl replied. "I confess to binge—watching....that is, when I'm not working..."

I tried to nudge into the conversation by way of changing the subject.

"What kind of work do you do?" I asked. My tactic worked! Carl turned to me, again holding my gaze with those big blues.

"I'm a private investigator. I'm in Miami just for this week, on a case."

"What kind of case?"

"Missing person," Carl said. He reached inside his shirt pocket.

"Actually, that's why I stopped in your shop."

He handed me his business card. "I should have identified myself that way, my apologies."

Bea had come out from where ever she'd disappeared to earlier and was busily serving the customers, scooping cones for several elderly ladies who must have come in while Carl, Jo and I were talking. I hadn't even noticed the customers. I was so caught up in the moment. I looked over at Bea and signaled if she needed me.

Bea caught my eye, gave a wink and a smile, and continued serving her customers. I turned to Carl.

"Do you think the person you are looking for might have come here?" I asked. For the first time I regretted not having installed security cameras. Uncle Ig never bothered. And in all the years Ig—Loo had called the Bayfront home, never had there been so much as a shoplifting incident let alone anything worse.

"We're always open," Jo added. "There's little we don't see."

"Do you have a security camera?"

Jo glanced at me. "It's on order. Mattie is the new owner here, she's updating everything..."

I mouthed a silent *thank—you* to Jo as Carl turned his attention to his satchel.

Carl opened the buckskin satchel and retrieved a small photograph.

"Her name is Sara Young," Carl said, handing me the photo. "She's from Pennsylvania. Technically, Sara is considered a runaway. She was a minor when she left Pennsylvania the month before last, but just a week ago she turned eighteen."

I watched enough true crime television to see where this was going.

"Now, by law, she is of legal age to go where she wanted. That's why it's only a technicality that she is a runaway..."

Peter nodded. "You're good, Miss Bryant!"

"Call me Mattie," I said, not caring how forward I sounded. I knew him all of ten minutes, but enough time to know that Carl Statler was a man I could see myself spending some time with. It was that simple. He was on a case. And he'd solve it. He wouldn't turn his back all because the runaway was now of age to run to the moon if she could. He'd not procrastinate. Carl would see it through. Carl was no Peter Dawson.

"Mattie," Carl nodded. "Thank you, *Mattie*. Call me Carl. So, you understand that Sara Young's parents are worried. They heard from her on her birthday, she called them and told them not to try to talk her into returning home. The call was traced to Florida. That's when I got involved."

"Yes, I'd be worried, too, if I were the parents," I said as I took another look at the photo.

Sara was lovely, her complexion make—up free and her long, light brown hair fell in a cascade of waves over her shoulders and down her arms.

Bea had finished serving the ladies, who were now waiting patiently at Jo's register to pay for their cones.

"I'll be right back," Jo said as she quickly excused herself.

Bea came around the display freezer and joined Carl and me. I handed her the photo of the beautiful runaway. Bea pegged her in seconds. "Good grief," she said, shaking her head. "Elfie looks so different without all the bling..."

Chapter 5

I came down with a killer summer bug and was holed up at home all week. Behind drawn curtains and closed doors I kept to myself while I nursed a headache an upset stomach, scratchy throat, sneezing, coughing, and, up until this morning, a fever to boot. When my temperature finally broke, I figured the worst was over. Still, I decided, I'll just keep myself at home another day or two to play it safe.

Bea and Jo kept Ig—Loo running and they called me every day. I wasn't surprised, then, when the phone rang as I was in the kitchen, fixing myself some breakfast. It sure felt good having an appetite again!

I didn't even bother to check my phone screen to see who was calling. It had to be Bea or Jo, no doubt. I gave a cheerful greeting. What I received back froze me in my tracks.

"Mathilde. I need to talk to you. It's very important. I cannot call anyone else."

Peter! The shrill whistle of the tea kettle on the stovetop jolted me out of my stupor. How long had it been since we last talked, two years? Three?

Don't freak out, Mattie, I ordered my lesser angel. I took the kettle off the burner. My hand shook as I poured the hot water into a cup.

Stay calm, don't give yourself a third degree burn over him. He's not worth it.

I took a deep breath and settled into a chair.

"Hello, Peter, what can I do for you?" I closed my eyes and braced for impact.

...

"He had some nerve calling you when he should be calling the cops!" Bea hissed.

After hearing Peter out, I paced the floors for two days. While I had planned to be home anyway, who knew it would be a case of going into hiding than waiting out the tail end of a nasty cold?

I didn't feel safe. And Peter would call again

from where ever he was. He'd been robbed, he told me. And someone was after him.

He did need me. I didn't want any part of the trouble he had gotten himself into. Still, I couldn't get him out of my head.

Thankfully, there were no customers to wait on since Ig—Loo wasn't open yet. Bea and I had the place to ourselves for the next half hour.

"Should I, Bea? Should I help him? He won't tell me where he is, but he says he needs an ally." I was beyond anger. I was suspended between my head and my heart. I couldn't pick a side, I told Bea. I was in limbo.

"You'll have trade—offs no matter what," Bea said. "If you agree to help him, you tie yourself up with him again, but this time, it will with a criminal element in the mix. On the other hand, if you choose to walk away, you know you're going to feel guilty, though I can't imagine why..."

She was right, of course.

"You still hang on to Peter in some way,

don't you, Mattie? Am I on to something here?"

Bea was more than onto something. She saw straight through me.

I could shed the engagement ring, but not the memories. But I had something else now. I was taking a new path and didn't want to make a wrong turn on it.

"I just don't know if I should get involved at the expense of Ig—Loo, Bea. We're just getting started. There's just so much to do. It's overwhelming..."

Bea frowned. "What more do we need to do, Mattie? Develop a wider menu? That's easy enough. Try out some new advertising gimmicks and hire some extra help to work outside spooning free samples?" Bea's frown suddenly melted as quickly as it had formed.

"Actually," she grinned, "giving out free ice cream samples could be fun. We could do customer taste tests!"

"Would that be fun for us, or for the people just looking for free stuff?"

Bea pulled an empty five—gallon ice cream container from the freezer and hoisted a replacement with the ease of someone who had done a fair share of heavy labor over the years.

"We'll make it so much fun, I bet the people will pay top dollar for a gallon or two of this when all is said and done!"

Bea's confidence made everything seem easy. Bea rubbed her hands hard and clapped them together several times, smiling.

"See? All done! Out with the old, in with the new! And that's what you've got to do, Mattie. Decide if you want to focus on Peter or on Ig— Loo. I'm with you either way, and I'm sure Jo will be, too."

We shared a one—minute—to—opening hug.

"Thanks, Bea, I really do need allies."

But so did Peter. And what worried me was that Carl came to us to help locate Sara Young. How much more thinly could I stretch myself?

"Believe in yourself, Mattie. Give yourself some credit." Bea walked around the counter. She unlocked the door, pulled up the window shade, and waved to a young couple with two toddlers in tow. The couple returned Bea's gesture but kept going.

"We'll get them on the way back!" Bea chuckled.

"Think so?" I asked.

"Feel so!" Bea answered brightly.

It was a no—brainer: Ig—Loo would be fine without me. The bigger question was whether I'd end up for better or for worse after helping Peter unload his wagon of woes.

Chapter 6

Why should you even care about Peter, Mattie? Aren't you busy enough with more important things? A *Mattie's Old Life versus Mattie's New Life* tug—of—war rolled around in my head so much the night before, I hardly, slept. Even Bea's pep talk hadn't totally turned me around. I was still stuck, Bea knew it, but I wasn't about to admit it out loud to anyone else. Especially to Carl Slater, who had worries of his own that were keeping him as stuck as I felt I was.

The dim lighting in the little café along the Bayside Marketplace promenade didn't help much when it came to reading the wine list, and it wasn't effective in casting a shadow over the concern in Carl Slater's eyes, either. I couldn't help but feel sorry for him. He was only doing his job, but he clearly felt trapped between a rock and a hard place, especially after it looked more and more like he was looking for two people instead of one, even if in name only.

I chose this quiet café as an alternative to bringing Carl back to Ig—Loo. As much as I could I wanted my business interests segregated from Carl's investigation. He'd asked me to meet with him to talk about Elfie.

Carl was waiting for me at a corner table when I arrived. He'd ordered us a carafe of Merlot. I'd have preferred Pinot Noir. Still, I went along for the ride. *Don't split hairs, Mattie,* I chided myself. *After all, who called whom? And it's not a date*! Carl got right to the point. For that, I was thankful. I wasn't in the mood for making small talk. I still had Peter on my mind, though Carl's good looks were a distraction. I couldn't concentrate on much of anything when those blue eyes of his bore into me like laser beams.

"Are you absolutely sure, Mattie, that the girl who entered your shop, who told you to call her Elfie, is my client's daughter? I know Bea is convinced that Elfie and Sara are the same girl. But are you and Joanne as certain?"

I nodded. "I see a keen likeness. That's the best way I can put it. I can't say I'm 'absolutely' sure. As for Joanne, she said she feels the same way I do, but you'd need to ask her directly."

Carl went on. "I'm looking for any leads from anyone who has seen both Sara and Elfie, which reminds me..." Carl handed me a few more of his business cards.

"Can you give Jo and Bea my card as well? I only left one with you and I'd hoped to be able to see both ladies tonight here with you."

I put the business cards in my purse and raised my glass of Merlot.

"To many more leads!" I said, a little too giddily.

Carl raised his glass to mine. "To part two of the overview. Let's stay focused, shall we?" He winked.

"I'm focused, Carl. I think your client's daughter is dangerous. I have no proof, only a feeling. And do you know why I trust my gut?" I didn't wait for his answer.

"It's because," I said, hoping I sounded confident. "I have a sixth sense."

"Smashing!" Carl exclaimed. "Just bloody smashing!"

"I agree, this Merlot is a smashingly fine vintage, Carl. Jolly good!" Or was it *bloody good? Mattie, don't pretend to be a Brit all because you're attracted to one!*

Carl gave me the longest stare anyone's given me since I refused to kill a beetle that had wandered into my classroom during my teaching days. The kids and I made the creature a home and let it live out its life on my desk in a kitchen match box. My principal thought I was nuts. Did Carl think I was nuts? An apology was in order, I felt.

"Sorry for butchering your accent, Carl. I really do love it. I just can't pull it off. But this wine...mmmm...so smooth and..."

Carl shook his head. "No. It's not that. I meant you, Mattie, *you* are smashing. Not the wine. I place as much weight on sixth senses as I do on hard facts. As for your 'British' accent, it's better than any southern drawl I can articulate. I'm happy to know you like my accent. In all my years here in sunny Florida, I never lost it." He smoothed his mustache with his fingers. "I kept the mustache and the accent!"

Peter had no mustache. "I was engaged to someone with a drawl," I said. Oddly, I felt fine getting this fact on record.

Carl's eyes widened. He raised his goblet to mine.

"*Was?*"

"Right. We never tied the knot."

Carl raised his goblet.

"To his loss, Mattie. Cheers!"

Carl had ordered food before I arrived. When he told me blooming onion and tip steak kabobs were on the way a memory surfaced, of Peter and me reading restaurant reviews of vegetarian eateries. In the end, we'd never try a place. Peter could never decide.

Maybe it was the Merlot. I loved being in Carl's company, yet thoughts of Peter and his ways got in the way. I found myself comparing Peter to Carl, and Carl to Peter. Another tug of war!

Hadn't Peter once told me that, when I enjoyed a glass or two of wine on an empty stomach, I tended to talk too much? Carl and I had polished off an entire carafe as I shared every detail I knew of Peter's troubles, past and present. Should I have done that?

Our server approached the table, his arms laden with plates. I couldn't wait to dig in. As I reached for a kabob, it fell from my hand onto my lap, then onto the floor beneath my chair. The server hurried to do damage control, kneeling on the tiled floor to retrieve the kabob, furiously wiping the floor of any sign of the accident.

"I will replace your kabob ma'am," the server said, rising to his feet. He offered a slight bow.

I was mortified. No. I was more than that. I was buzzed.

Carl didn't miss a beat. He turned to the server.

"Could you also bring coffee? Make it black, please."

Carl settled back in his chair. "Let's change the subject. We've talked almost all evening about my investigation. What are Bea and Joanne up to this evening while we're here?"

I didn't want to compromise what Jo was doing. Ig—Loo and all things related to ice cream, and Jo's decision to do some recon on her own, all of this was off limits. While I was sitting in this café with Carl, eating up his compliments—and his dinner selections (the man has excellent taste, did I mention that?)— and making a fool of myself in my buzzed state, Joanne was scrutinizing Tasty Glacier's floor—to—ceiling menu with a fine-tooth comb. The last time we'd talked, Joanne made clear what she intended to do.

Mattie, as the gods are my witnesses, if I

have to stay at Tasty Glacier until closing and pretend I'm waiting for my no—show date, I'll copy every line of that floor—to—ceiling digital menu. I just wish phone cameras were not so obvious. But I'm bringing a puzzle book along to hide behind while I write.

Joanne Blake was nothing if not a woman of her word. I promised Jo I'd call her first thing the next day for a debriefing on the results of her mission.

"Bea's doing the books tonight," I answered Carl, truthfully.

"What about Joanne? Did she work home, too?

Look at him, not at your dinner napkin, Mattie. I gave Carl my best *I feel mellow* smile as our eyes met.

"I think she planned on meeting up with some people in Coconut Grove," I said, hoping I was convincing. It was as close to telling the truth as I could manage without blowing Jo's cover.

Carl leaned back in his chair. "Ah. Well,

another time, hopefully." he said.

"What do you mean?" His comment sounded like an opportunity missed but, missed for what? I gulped my coffee. I wasn't keeping up with this conversation. And I sure wasn't prepared for Carl's answer to my question.

"I liked Bea and Joanne the moment I met them," he said. "We would have enjoyed ourselves, the four of us, sitting around this table tonight, feasting and toasting and chatting about this and that..."

That stung! Wasn't my company good enough? Weren't we enjoying the evening, just the two of us at the table, chatting about, well, *who is whom*? Okay, so I got a bit tipsy. And I dropped a kabob. But this was a *working* meetup, wasn't it? At least it had started out that way. *And it is still a working meetup. Remember, Mattie, you're here on business, not on a date! Maybe Carl needs a social life, but you don't. Your dance card is full...of work.*

As the rich black coffee finally got to work

clearing my head, I remembered that talk I'd had with Bea and how it just might be possible for me to successfully to juggle all the responsibilities that came with running Ig—Loo and, at the same time, help someone in need.

We *could* have an evening out with Bea and Jo, all four of us, that is, when we weren't all going in different directions at the same time!

But Carl was right about them. Bea and Jo were likeable from the get—go. And even more, what would I do without them at Ig—Loo? What would I do without their trust and friendship? They were more than employees, they were family. I wondered, maybe that's why Carl likes Bea and Jo. They must make him feel at home here in South Florida. Was there someone in Gainesville waiting for him to get back? And what about his native England! Had he left a sweetheart behind when he'd come to the States for college, then decided to stay here?

Carl's circumstances match mine, I thought.

No wedding ring on his finger, his daily routine devoted to work, and now, alone in Miami while he worked a case. But I was here because it was my home, my city. I had most of my friends and family close by. Carl was truly alone.

I finished my coffee and watched Carl pay the check. He needs an anchor, I felt, and we were it. Bea, Joanne and yours truly had become Carl's family by proxy.

Carl was pulling out his credit card and here I was, the buzz gone and replaced by day dreaming and conjectures. I couldn't wait to be of help to Carl yet here I was, not even offering to help him with our working—supper bill.

I reached for my purse. "Let me chip in, Carl."

Carl waved off my gesture and smiled as he helped me up from my chair. "My treat," he winked.

Oh, those eyes!

We left the café and took in the cool evening

breezes off Biscayne Bay. I felt much better since overdoing it with the wine. My thoughts were clear, and I assured Carl that I was glad he liked Bea and Jo as much as I did.

"Let's invite Bea and Jo to come with us the next time we go out" I said, immediately regretting how eager I sounded. My face suddenly felt hot. I hadn't meant to assume there *was* a "next time" on the social horizon. Not outwardly, anyway!

Carl's eyes widened. He reached for my hand and squeezed it warmly.

"I'd like that, Mattie. And I especially like spending time with *you*. Hope your sixth sense feels it."

We held hands until we reached the edge of the Bayside Market Place where traffic of busy Biscayne Boulevard invited a quick sprint on the pedestrian green light.

By the time Carl and I bid each other good night and went our separate ways, I realized I was getting in over my head, caring not only about Peter and what happened to him, but caring for Carl too, in his lonely search for a runaway.

Maybe I could help both of them find the people they were looking for, and still manage to grow Ig—Loo. Stretching my time like that, pulling myself in different directions that couldn't possibly benefit me defied logic. But my sixth sense told me to go with it.

Chapter 7

Dear Mattie,

You must know that saying: Let no good deed go un—punished. There's some truth to that because I'm living proof of it. What I told you over the phone was not the whole story. I left out some messy details that make me look stupid. But Mattie, I can't keep this to myself, especially if something goes wrong and either I can't return to Miami, or I'm sent back in handcuffs.

This girl I met, Sally, who I tried to help, took off, but not before she accused me of stalking her, of forcing her to spend the night with me against her will. She posted the accusations on her social media. Two police officers came to my door. I thought they were responding to my 911 call. They said no, that they were dispatched to follow up on a call that had been made ABOUT me, not FROM me.

That's what I get for feeling sorry for Sally

and giving her a place to stay until I could help her get home. It was all a ruse. I fell for her sob story about being stranded in Miami, about losing her phone and wallet on the metro. Then it was drizzling outside, I couldn't just let her stand in the rain with no place to go.

What a sucker I was. The worst this is, Sally didn't just steal money from me, she took off with our diamond engagement ring, Mattie. It was locked up tight as a drum since you gave it back to me, but Sally found it anyway.

Sally's a pro, Mattie. She told me she was from Key West. I'm going down there.

Mattie, I wouldn't blame you if you don't care, you don't owe me anything. I know I let you down. I just need you to know what I'm up against, just in case something happens to me.

Peter

My whole body trembled as I called Bea. I read that letter three times and still couldn't believe it. Peter was being blackmailed; I was sure of it! Didn't he see that? Why would he be accused of a crime by someone who had already robbed him and had taken off?

Bea, flabbergasted, had the same question.

"And why on earth did Peter *snail mail* the letter?" she added. "An entire day, maybe two days, wasted while it was going through the postal maze!"

I wondered the same thing. "What does it mean, Bea? Why didn't Peter just pick up the phone and call me back? Why the paper trail?"

Bea sighed into the receiver. "It makes no sense, Mattie. Should I let Joanne know about this or are you going to wait to tell her when you call her anyway?"

"Call her anyway?" I echoed. My head was spinning. "About what, Bea?"

"Jo said she was waiting for your call, you know, about her little foray," Bea answered.

Joanne! Her recon mission to The Tasty Glacier! I'd completely forgotten to touch base with her as I'd promised. *That's some pathetic example of proving you could juggle more than one ball at a time, Mattie!* Two days had gone by since Carl and I had met up at the café. I'd left a message, just to thank him again for the dinner. When he didn't get back to me, I admit I felt a little deflated. He must be very busy, I reasoned. We'd catch up at some point. I scoured Peter's letter again. *Now this.*

"Mattie? Are you still there?"

I took a deep breath. *One thing at a time, Mattie.*

"I'm here, Bea. Yes, go ahead and fill Joanne in on all of this. Oh, and please let her know I'll go over her findings from the Tasty Glacier as soon as I can, and we'll start ordering the flavors we decide on, of course with different names, oh and..."

"No need, Mattie," Bea broke in.

"What do you mean 'no need'?"

Again, Bea sighed through the phone and I braced myself for more bad news, though what else could go wrong today eluded me.

I think it can wait 'til I see you," Bea said.

"Is it Aunt Loo? Uncle Ig? Is there trouble in paradise?"

The last postcard I'd received from Aunt Loo, was literally *with love from Aunt Loo*. Not from *Aunt Loo and Uncle Ig*.

"No. I'm sure they're fine." Bea said, no doubt trying to reassure me. She'd noticed the absence of Uncle Ig's name on the postcard, too, when I read the card to her and Jo.

"Then what, Bea? I'm running in circles and..."

Bea broke in, "Precisely! That's why Jo and I took some matters into our own hands when we saw how busy you were with Carl Statler...."

Was my attraction to Carl that obvious? I had to set Bea straight.

"We're busy, yes, but Carl thought you and Jo were going to join us at the café. And besides, it's not like I've never been with a nice-looking man. But it was a meeting over dinner, Bea, not a date." I felt my cheeks flush in spite of my assurance to Bea that Carl and I were all about business.

Bea chuckled. "Oh, Mattie, I didn't mean *that* kind of busy. Okay, I'll fill you in right now. After Jo got back from Tasty Glacier, she and I went over the flavor names she gathered from their menu. She got all of them, Mattie, a treasure trove of ideas for jazzing up the names of Ig—Loo's flavors. Jo called our supplier. Turns out we can get most of those flavors in generic descriptions. Jo found out that we can jazz up the generic names and it would not be misleading or illegal. It's just good, creative business. If Tasty could do it, we could, too, if it's okay with you. Jo and I don't mind doing the legwork. We just need your blessing. Ig— Loo is your baby. We're just the sitters."

For the umpteenth time, I sent up a prayer of thanks for Bea's clearheaded attention to Ig—Loo, and for Jo's willingness to use the better part of her time off to essentially work for free. I was preoccupied not only with Peter's troubles but with feelings bubbling up inside of me every time I thought of Carl. I couldn't admit these feelings to Bea or Jo, not yet, though it seemed that Bea had figured out at least some of what was going on with me. Still, the last thing Bea and Jo needed was an ice cream shop proprietor who had more stars in her eyes for a handsome Brit than for the much—needed growth spurt Ig—Loo was about to reveal to the public, thanks to their hard work. Bea and Jo had saved Ig—Loo from getting lost in the competitive wave of trendy stops and eateries along the Bayfront of one of the most popular destination spots in South Florida. They certainly did more for Ig—Loo that I'd done in the months since Aunt Loo and Uncle Ig passed the baton to me. Shoot, I'd once considered employing Elfie just for a public relations boost! Who was a bigger fool, Peter Dawson or yours truly?

I soaked up Bea's words as she ran off the names she and Jo had given to Ig—Loo's forthcoming new and exciting flavor offerings.

"We now have Passion Fruit 'n Nut,

Marshmallow Mint, Cheery Choco—Cherry, Blueberry Crème Brule, Peanut Brittle Burst, and Rum Runner Raisin on our menu!" Bea all but broke into song over the phone.

"It's all good, Bea!" I assured her. "When is the shipment arriving? After all you two have done for me, I want to at least show up to help stock our freezer."

"Again, no need Mattie, the order arrived bright and early this morning. We were already here. Jo and I put everything in place, even put up the bigger menu board. It's not as big as Tasty Glacier's, but it's doing a good job showing us off!"

"I've got to take you two out on the town one night after work. It's the least I can do after all you've done for Ig—Loo," I offered.

"Offer accepted," Bea replied. "We've missed you, Mattie."

Ouch! And I had felt stung when Carl mentioned how he hoped we could all get together socially one of these days. Were Jo and Bea stung because I hadn't been around much to help expand Ig—Loo?

"I'm really sorry, Bea. I haven't done my fair share. That changes as soon. Are you and Jo angry with me?"

"Of course not! Just share Peter's letter with Carl today if you can," Bea urged. "Carl may be able to help find Peter's runaway thief while he's still looking for Sara Young. Kill two runaway birds with one P.I. stone, you could say!"

Bea's analysis put a smile on my face. How helpful she was, putting a positive and humorous spin on things just when I needed a lift!

"And won't it be nice," she added, "not having to spend our evenings slinking around in the Grove, sizing up our competition!"

I couldn't have said it better myself. Bea signed off with the promise that she and Jo would hold the fort at Ig—Loo. I was alone again, with only Peter's words on paper for company. I folded the letter and placed it back in its envelope. Something this important, snail mailed. Why? So much time wasted. Bea saw right away that something wasn't right with this. And when I read Peter's letter to her, she hadn't displayed any emotion or worry for him. But why would she? Bea and Jo, my Aunt Loo and Uncle Ig, shoot, even my parents thought I was right to cut the cord where Peter Dawson was concerned. Was I still hanging on by a thread to the idea that maybe Peter and I weren't as finished as I'd made clear when I took the engagement ring off my finger, and when he sighed with relief that I'd done so?

Stop beating a dead horse, Mattie. Get dressed, find Carl, show him Peter's letter. Then get back to Ig—Loo where you belong!

Chapter 8

Carl agreed to meet up on the Bayfront. When I finally reached him, I told him I'd bring him back to Ig—Loo to say hi to Bea and Jo and sample some of Ig—Loo's new flavors, but that first and foremost, I had to see him alone.

I headed for the promenade, made a left toward the tourist ferries, and there he was, just where Bea told me to look. Earlier, on her way back to Ig—Loo from her lunch break, Bayfront, Bea saw him watching a ferry boat filled with tourists pull out of its slip.

"He's got flowers!" Bea had squealed as she adjusted her visor and took my place behind the freezer. "Go now, before he gives them to somebody else! Oh, and take this! Jo added two spoons." Bea handed me a paper bag. *Rum Runner Raisin* was neatly printed on the folded flap.

Bea winked through her specs, "If it hadn't been for the Double R, where'd we be?"

I blew kisses to both ladies. "You two are the best! See you after lunch!"

Rushing out the door, my budding feelings for Carl were exposed to the world to see. I could have slowed my pace, but why should I? I didn't want the ice cream to melt! *Your turn to wink, Mattie!*

I was so happy to see Carl that I practically threw myself, into his outstretched arms, arms that, true to Bea's words, held a mixed bouquet of beautiful blooms.

"These are for you, I hope you like cut flowers." Carl said smiling as he handed me the wrapped bouquet. (Did I like cut flowers? Is there any other kind? The only flowers I can handle are cut ones! Some people have a green thumb. I have a lethal one.)

I buried my nose in the bouquet. The variety of fragrances was intoxicating. "I adore cut flowers, Carl! Thank you!" I handed him the bag.

"We have some new flavors!" I pointed out

the name on the bag's flap.

Carl read it and smiled broadly. "What a cool name! Is there real rum in it?"

I laughed in spite of myself, remembering our partaking of the spirits at the café. "No, Ig—Loo doesn't have a liquor license! Actually, we have a dozen new flavors."

Carl opened the bag. He took out the two plastic spoons. A sly smile escaped from beneath his mustache. His blue eyes twinkled.

"Do all the new flavors all come with *two* spoons?" Carl asked, handing one to me. He found an open space on the crowded bay wall.

"I think we can fit us here," he said, gesturing me to sit first. He then squeezed in beside me.

Sitting so close to Carl, I felt like a teenager on her first date.

Silently, I gave myself marching orders: *Mattie, you're here to give Carl the letter from Peter, not to flirt over faux—spiked ice cream!*

The ice cream was heavenly and, indulging with Carl, our little our plastic spoons dipping and weaving through the paper container, touching, clicking, competing for who gets the most raisins this time was, for me at least, heaven on Earth. I might have forgotten Peter's letter had Carl not beat me to the last raisin. He wiped both our chins with a paper napkin and took a deep, satisfying breath.

"Mattie, I've never enjoyed dessert before lunch so much as I have today! Was that really why you wanted to meet up? Was I recruited to rate one of Ig—Loo's newest flavors? If so, I give Rum Runner Raisin five stars!"

The last thing I wanted to do was put a damper on the moment. I wanted to spend all afternoon with Carl. I wanted to hold onto my bouquet, take his arm and promenade along the Bayfront, pretending that he and I were walking down the aisle as man and wife, to live happily together always. I wanted...

Carl gently tapped my shoulder, breaking into my quiet daydream.

"Five stars not good enough? Okay then, make it six. Six stars for Rum Runner Raisin.

The sky's the limit!"

"I'm sorry, Carl, I was somewhere out there."
I gestured to beautiful Biscayne Bay. I was
stalling, knowing I needed to get to the point,
to give him that letter. I continued to gaze at
the sparkling waters of the bay. I wondered
what would have happened had Aunt Loo and
Uncle Igor never left Miami, if Elfie had shown
up when *they* were behind the freezer tending
to customers.

Maybe Aunt Loo would have sent Elfie away:
*Young lady, it's not even three o'clock. Are you
cutting class?* Uncle Igor, I was sure, would
have not given a thought to the possibility that
a teenager might be skipping school in search
of some good old fashioned ice cream—infused
hooky playing. Nope, Uncle Igor would have
piled as many scoops as he could onto sugar
cone, given it to Elfie for free, just as Bea had
done, and invited her back any time.
Suddenly, I missed my aunt and uncle more
than ever. What would they do if they were in
my shoes?

I wished my Aunt Loo were here, instead of learning how to line dance at a senior—only RV park in Arizona, so that she could be Uncle Igor's partner "on every occasion" as her most recent post card revealed.

Carl wrapped his hand around mine, bringing me back to the here and now. "C'mon, let's stroll a bit."

We walked the promenade. Carl was in a chatty mood.

"I haven't seen much of Miami since I got here, Mattie. I took the 'Famous Celebrities' Houses' ferry tour. When I put myself back on the clock, I checked all my messages. I counted three calls from you and just as I was getting ready to call you back, my phone rang and there you were again! And now…"

I checked my watch. Jo would be waiting for me to relieve her for lunch.

"I wish I could stay longer," I interrupted. I fished through my purse, balancing the bouquet. Carl took the bouquet. "Take your time. What are you looking for?"

I retrieved Peter's letter from my purse and held it out to Carl.

"Before I go back to work, please, Carl, read this. He sent it by *snail mail*, if you can believe it! I just received it. He could have emailed. He could have called. Do you think he did that just to give himself time to put distance between himself and the rest of us?"

"Back up, Mattie," Carl said. "Who's 'he'?" He handed me back my bouquet and opened the letter.

I cradled the beautiful flowers in my arms as though they were a living thing, even though the moment the shears separated them from their roots, they were beyond need of nurturing. Still, the flowers were all I would have left of Carl once he finished reading Peter's letter. I felt sure he'd try to help, but it would mean being away longer, trying to find not one but two runaways.

Before I could answer, Carl started reading aloud, then turned stone silent as his eyes followed Peter's words on the page. When he finished, his face was ashen. His eyes met mine, resolute. They told me everything.

"Mattie, I'm going to Key West to find my clients' daughter once and for all. I know she's down there. I have two leads now."

"What do you mean, *two* leads?" I asked.

"This," Carl held up Peter's letter, "and a message I received that I picked up late when I took time off to be a tourist."

"I don't understand."

Carl turned to face the bay. Couldn't he look me in the eyes? He spoke so softly I had to ask him to repeat himself.

"A man left a voice message at my office in Gainesville. I picked it up this morning. He said he needed help locating someone named Sally who had run away from his house in Miami with stolen goods and threatened him. He wanted to know if I could take the case, and if I could meet him in Key West, that's where he was going."

Carl turned his gaze from the bay back to

the letter. He tapped the paper softly.

"He said he didn't want police involved, Mattie. The message sounded like a man in trouble, just like this letter writer, Peter, sounds. The man who called my office gave his full name. Peter Dawson. Could it..."

Carl's eyes searched mine, his mouth moving, speaking words I no longer heard.

My knees buckled. Sirens went off in my ears. I leaned hard against Carl's chest, my bouquet crushed between us. Carl led us to a private spot near a grassy area away from the promenade, easing me into a low bench. Everything was moving in slow motion.

"Just take a deep breath, Mattie. Take your time."

His eyes searched my face. He looked scared. I leaned against his shoulder.

"I'm okay, Carl, really. I'm not going to faint..."

Chapter 9

Joanne said I was out cold. Much later, I remembered my flowers. What happened to them?

Just before everything went black, an onslaught of questions had run rampant through my mind and erupted like a volcano. *How did Peter know about Carl? Had Peter been following us? Had he lurked around Bayside Market like a spy in the night as we left the café? Could Carl find out if Sara Young and Peter knew each other all along?*

Was Peter was trying to get back at me for leaving him? Was he creating a scenario, playing the victim so that I would feel bad for him? And what was all this "our diamond" talk?

Joanne said she'd found Carl holding me while a small group had gathered, some on their phones. Carl was frantic, Jo said, pleading for an ambulance, asking if there was a doctor nearby, begging me to wake up. At first, I only had Joanne's recount of what had happened to me. I had none of my own details to offer when I finally woke up in the emergency room, surrounded by people in scrubs, all of them knowing my name and asking me if I knew it, too. How long was I out, an hour, or a day? I couldn't put any of the pieces together.

Then slowly, I began to remember things. I had screamed. Someone put an oxygen mask over my nose and mouth. I remembered Carl bringing my fingers to his lips, his eyes on the tube bandaged to my wrist, suspended from a plastic bag hanging above my bed.

Elfie. Peter. I remembered them, but why? I called for Carl.

He was sleeping on a chair in my room.

I'm here, Mattie. I'm not going until the doctors say I have to.

My bed moved. Someone was wheeling it away. I was going somewhere. I was leaving Carl.

Find them, Carl...get them....

I felt another mask on my face. Then my world went black again.

...

Aunt Loo was on a roll as she kept me company in my room at South Miami Hospital.

"Bea practically jumped over the freezer and Joanne completely forgot the customer she was ringing up on the register! They just could not believe I was back. 'And not just for a visit,' I told them! This traveler is back to stay!"

My Aunt Loo's return to Miami shocked me too, that is, if I could have been any more shocked after waking up from what the doctors calmly assured me was just a bit of stress, a chain reaction that had caused *temporary melt—away* and subsequent loss of consciousness. I'd never heard of such a thing. A nervous breakdown or an anxiety attack, yes. But a temporary melt—away? That wasn't a diagnosis. It was more like variation on *"Goin' Fruity"* a name Jo christened one of Ig—Loo's new flavors.

When Aunt Loo appeared at my bedside, I'd thought I'd dreamt the whole thing.

"Carl Statler, the man who you are working with, contacted your Uncle Igor and me and told us what happened. Your folks also know. They were here last night but you were sleeping."

I hadn't spoken much with mom and dad since taking over Ig—Loo. I tried calling once a week, but it didn't stick. They'd visited Ig—Loo a few times, enjoyed a few cones, and I also sent them home with extra quarts of their old favorite, Chocolate Chip Mint, on Ig—Loo's tab. But I couldn't remember the last time I'd actually visited them on a Sunday afternoon, just to shoot the breeze over a meal, or take in a movie together in town like we use to do. Hanging with my folks seemed like a long—ago tradition no longer held in the Bryant household. Yet, they were here at the hospital when I was flat on my back. *What lousy timing, Mattie. Couldn't you stay awake for your own folks?*

"Will they be stopping in again?" I asked, hoping for a second chance to see them and have a long overdue chat, even if it had to be from a hospital bed.

My aunt assured me they would be back. "Everybody wants to see you, honey." Then I asked about Uncle Ig. Those two never traveled without the other in tow, but he wasn't with her today.

Aunt Loo let out such a long, full breath, it was as if she'd just come up for air after a free dive.

"Your uncle isn't here, Mattie. I guess I'd better hit the nail on the head. Igor was foot dragging, so I took it upon myself to head back to Miami."

I noticed the third finger on her left hand was naked.

"Where's your wedding band? Did you two have a fight or something?" I tried to shift to a more comfortable sitting position in my hospital bed. Aunt Loo jumped up and plumped my pillows.

"Don't twist, honey, I'll help you, and yes, we had it out!" Aunt Loo pulled her chair, pulling it closer to the bed. She leaned over the safety rail.

"Igor promised me we'd take the RV up to Alaska," she whispered as though someone else might hear. "But he kept putting it off. I did more line dancing than I wanted to in the Southwest. It was time to go. But then I found out about this bimbo, some waitress named Melanie, big hair, big *everything.*" Aunt Loo patted her bodice, then her hips, shaking her head.

I couldn't imagine my uncle going after another woman. He was over the moon about Aunt Loo, even after decades of marriage.

"Maybe this *bimbo* had made a move on *him*," I suggested, my own voice a whisper now.

Aunt Loo bristled, "No. I'm sure she didn't lure him into our RV. Igor had to have invited her in. I found them together!"

"What were they doing?" I asked, dreading the answer even as I probed for one.

"What do you *think*, Mattie?" my aunt huffed as she practically flew out of her chair. "They were doing *this*!" Her hands went to her hips as she kicked one cowgirl boot—clad foot forward, perched on her toes with the other foot, and executed a seamless quarter—pivot.

"Uncle Igor and the bimbo were *line dancing*?"

Aunt Loo shot me a long, slow nod as she ran a manicured nail around the spot on her ring finger where her wedding band used to sit.

"If your uncle thought he could pull one over on me, he has another thing coming! He wanted to stick around in Arizona because of her! He always wanted to dance with her! The RV park was having a line dance competition, and first prize was a whole week of free camping! I quote, 'We won't head up to Alaska, Loo, until we enter the contest!' That's what your uncle told me, and under no uncertain terms. He was so hard—nosed about it! His way or no way! What got into him, I can't say for sure, but I have a feeling he was just trying to play Mister Big Boss to impress the bimbo! When I told him I didn't think we'd win, he recruited that woman! The nerve! So, I started practicing really hard, even wrote you about it, did you get my card?"

"Yes, you wrote that you were going to be Uncle Ig's *'partner for all occasions'*." I reached over the bed rail to give her a hug. She indulged me, but just for a split second.

"Oh, I'm a partner, all right, a *sucker* of a partner!" she huffed, pulling back.

"What do you mean?" I asked

"I'll tell you what I mean! Your uncle *still chose Miss Bimbo* as his dance partner for the contest. Even with all my practicing, he said it was too late, that they already had a routine memorized, and two dress rehearsals, and, well...here I am....he's dancing his life away and I have been replaced as his partner for all occasions...." I never saw Aunt Loo so close to tears as she looked then. I was stricken. I saw myself in her eyes.

"Good grief, Aunt Loo, you sound like me! That's exactly how I felt when ..." *Peter!* My aunt had succeeded in distracting me from thinking about Peter, and, up 'til now, she'd done such a good job! But she pulled at a common thread. Or had she? Peter and I *didn't* get married. I had no husband because *I'd never* had a husband. But Aunt Loo and Uncle Ig *had* married. Were *still* married, and really, were *more* than just married. They were stuck like glue to each other.

Aunt Loo was pacing around my bed now.

"I called an Uber to take me to the airport and got the first flight out on a standby ticket, Mattie. I took off my wedding ring to go through TSA. It's in my bag. But I have to say, my dear, that right now I'm so mad at Igor, I don't even want to wear it!"

Listening to Aunt Loo, part of me wanted to commiserate, but another part of me wanted to tell her to put that wedding ring on, fly back to Arizona, and sweep Uncle Ig off his dancing feet. Alaska wasn't going anywhere. And neither was my uncle going any place without Aunt Loo. As I saw it, Uncle Ig just teamed up with the lady at the RV park because she was evidently one heck of a line dancer. Aunt Loo didn't think she and Uncle Ig would be a winning ticket on the sawdust, so the *bimbo* became Uncle Ig's Plan B. My uncle hadn't even locked their RV when he and his fill—in partner were inside doing their moves...their *dance* moves!

"That's some hot mess, Aunt Loo! But you know, I think you would have won that contest. Look at you!" I said, giving my own feet a few little kicks from under the hospital blanket to make my point. "You can line dance with the best of the bimbos!" I tried my best to keep it light, for her sake. Aunt Loo was clearly on overload just like I had been the last time I saw Carl, when he'd held me as my volcano erupted, as I melted away.

I closed my eyes as my aunt talked on, first pushing back on my suggestion that she might have offered some stiff competition to the line dance contestants, and then musing *maybe I was too hasty...*

Suddenly I felt so tired. Carl and Peter, Elfie, even Ig—Loo, all seemed brushed over in the whirlwind called Aunt Loo. She had swept into town, elbowed my problems out of the room and helped me forget for a while that I wasn't the only one with a full plate of woes.

Still, my aunt's problems could be untangled with a phone call and a return plane ticket to Arizona. Mine were still in a knotted jumble, most likely somewhere on the streets of Key West.

Louise "Loo" Bryant and I were family, Floridians to the bone, but, unlike my well—traveled aunt, I'd never once visited Key West.

I wanted her to return to Arizona and fix the misunderstanding with Uncle Igor. He hadn't been foot dragging. She had just been uncompromising, like I'd become since shedding Peter.

Maybe it was high time I practiced what I preached.

Chapter 10

"You know something, Mattie? Your aunt channels you. She even looks like you," Jo said as she wiped down the freezer. I nodded as I ran a floor mop over Ig—Loo's brand new, ice blue colored ceramic tiles, picking up sneaker and flip—flop shoe prints left by the throngs of customers that had kept us busy non—stop for most of the day. As mobbed with customers as we were all day, I could tell Jo had something on her mind. And——who was I kidding——so did I.

It was just Jo and yours truly behind the freezer and at the register all day. Bea was off, taking a much-deserved break from work to visit her daughter in Hialeah. As we began the nightly clean—up, Jo played amateur shrink. She's pretty good at it, actually!

Let her psyche you out, Mattie. Just mop and breathe.

Jo pulled off her plastic gloves and skirted

the freezer, her hands on her hips. I kept mopping but gave her a quick smile.

"Jo, could you stand over there?" I pointed to a spot on the floor that was still waiting for my mop. "You might slip on the wet tiles. Then I'd have flashbacks of the melt away I took last month."

Moving to where I pointed, Jo huffed and turned her head. She watched the foot traffic visible beyond the CLOSED sign in the window, but I knew better. Jo wasn't regretting our closing an hour early and missing potential customers. She had something to say and it was time for her to say it. I kept mopping. *Patience, Mattie.* Finally, in true Jo fashion, she ticked off the facts as she saw them.

"Okay, so now you are safe from your aunt's influences. Your doctor gave you a clean bill of health, your friends and family, even Carl Statler, stopped everything to be there for you, are *still* there for you, and now you are back at work. And you have no flashbacks."

Jo's tone hinted that she was on her way to layering these points with a dose of drama only she could pull off: the kind that made everything even more logical when all was said and done. Once Jo was out of preamble mode, she was loud as a firecracker.

Here it comes, Mattie!

She swung around and faced me. One look at her furrowed brow, beet red cheeks and quivering chin, and I knew what was next. *Okay, Jo, let it rip.* And rip she did.

"Loo Bryant may only be related to you by her marriage to your uncle, but you and she could be twins! Inside and out! Same unruly brown hair, same hazel eyes, same too—much—around—the—hips, and oh don't let me forget, that fighting spirit once you decide you've had enough of something! You and Loo even think and feel the same way when it comes to the men in your lives!"

Jo's rant stopped me in mid—mop up. *Whoa! Where are you taking this, Jo?* This little psych session was getting out of hand. I called for a time out.

"Hold on, Jo! Louise and Igor Bryant have *always* been in it for the long haul. They are in love. Like kids at the prom! They *never* got tired of each other. But I got tired of Peter because I was fed up with *waiting*. Who proposes and buys a ring then won't commit to a wedding date? No, Jo, that's where any similarities between my aunt and I part ways. Look how fast she flew back to Arizona after she and my uncle talked it out? I mean, sure, she waited until I was out of the hospital to talk with him, but she called him!"

"*He* called *her*," Jo retorted. "Loo was all set to move in with you and start working here again to help out while you got your strength back! She said so herself!"

Jo was right. Just comparing my history with Peter to that of my aunt and uncle's relationship was enough to make my head spin.

"I stand corrected, Jo, I'm so befuddled...it's been such a rough ride."

I wasn't in the mood to argue the fine points of relationships, mine or others. The doctors told me not to overload, to work on moving forward as I'd been doing since leaving Peter and changing careers. I'd even started attending an informal support group once a week with other young professional business owners who, like me, were finding their way, distinguishing want, from need. Wasn't there a song about that a long time ago? My parents use to play it on the old stereo when I was young.

I was thinking more about my parents, and our happy times together that I'd all but forgotten in my mad dash to make some kind of mark. Now I was making good on my word to touch base with them more regularly. I felt better just knowing they were there, just like my aunt and uncle, and Joanne and Bea were there. So many good people were cheering me on.

Maybe Carl was, too.

Jo had moved off the dry spot I'd asked her

to take. She stood squarely in front of me now, shaking my mop handle.

"Hey, Earth to Mattie! What's the matter?" she asked, snapping her fingers at me. I blinked.

"Nothing, Jo, I'm sorry! I just was thinking..." And then it hit me. I knew what I needed to do. I turned to Jo and handed her the mop.

"Can you finish up here for me?"

Jo squinted. "Sure, but we were talking..."

"I know, Jo," I interrupted. "Aunt Loo. We were talking about her. Look, Jo, my aunt was just talking off the top of her head. Nothing could keep her away from Uncle Ig, not even some line dancer at an RV park. And the way I see it, Jo, the *bimbo* wasn't even a threat to begin with."

Jo shrugged. "Well, I agree, Mattie, but..."

"I'm thinking seriously of going to Key West," I blurted.

Jo's squint turned pop—eyed and the grin that broke out on her face said it all. Jo knew, too. She'd probably known what was going in my head before I did.

"Find him, Mattie," Jo said. "Go with Carl and find Peter. You know you need to do that. You need to help them both."

"I know."

"Carl didn't want to leave you. Nobody's seen Sara Young, Elfie, or Peter here on the Bayfront. Carl is re-checking leads here, but he has to move on. There's nothing new here."

There she was, "Doctor" Joanne Blake at her finest.

For all the drama, she made perfect sense.

"Would you and Bea mind handling things here, again, without me?"

Jo gave me a look that reminded me that I was preaching to the choir.

"We'll handle Ig—Loo," Jo assured me. "Business is booming thanks to our expanded menu and new look. If we have to, Bea and I can recruit for some help, maybe someone to give out samples of our flavor of the week on Freebie Wednesdays."

Jo's idea to dedicate one day a week to pitching one of Ig—Loo's new tastes was something even Tasty Glacier hadn't done!

"As long as you and Bea hire help we can trust, I'm fine with that."

"And they *must* conform to Ig—Loo's dress code," Jo added.

"Absolutely," I said, "or else...."

We both knew what that condition implied: *If Elfie showed her face or her fascinator at Ig—Loo again, there was going to be trouble.*

Jo shooed me with her free hand as she dipped the mop into the bucket of sudsy water.

"Now, get out of here, Mattie," "I've got this. Go down to the Keys, and help that man of yours," she said, then winked.

"Whichever man it is, that is!"

Joanne Blake, you read my mind again!

Chapter 11

Carl's gaze was fixed on my hands. "Do you always grip your armrests with such passion?"

Passion? Don't you mean panic?

"Yes," I answered between my clenched teeth.

"And why is that?" Carl asked as another stretch of turbulence rocked the small commuter prop plane. Raindrops slapped against the tiny cabin windows then flattened into thin water slivers that resembled lines of thread moving diagonally along the glass against the heavy, grey cloud cover hovering above the Keys. We were flying directly into "a weather event" as the pros say. I'd wanted to drive down, but Carl had planned to fly to save time. He had also anticipated that I would want to come along. I closed my eyes and recalled the past few hours that resulted in my being on an airplane for the first time in my life.

Carl had sent me a text: *I have a ticket for you. Meet me at the airport. We've got an 8AM flight to Key West. Be at Terminal C by seven at latest. I'll be there.*

When Carl and I met up at the airport, I'd asked him how he'd read my mind.

"I didn't, actually," he admitted. "Joanne called me last night. She said you wanted to go to Key West with me, that you wanted to help. She knew I was still in town somewhere, so she didn't bother leaving a message with the answering service in Gainesville. She called my mobile number instead. I've been on the streets a lot, putting in a slew of hours retracing old leads, coming up empty every time. Still..." Carl squeezed my hand and laughed, recalling how he handed me his business card on the first day he'd stopped into Ig—Loo, then two more, for Jo and Bea, at the café.

"My little cards may appear old fashioned in this day and age what with all the digital technology, but I'm glad Jo had one. It pays to have some business cards flying about, but..."

Flying about! Ouch! It was time to change the subject, I'd decided then and there.

"I wonder if Elfie—I mean, Sara, really went to Key West."

Carl shrugged, "We'll do the best we can to find her. Peter, too. Sara's business is legitimate, by the way. But it's fluid."

"What do you mean, 'fluid'?"

"My clients, Sara's parents, told me Sara does run her own business. She designs, makes and sells her one-of-a-kind fashion accessories. But she's not online, has no business cards, nothing brick and mortar to speak of..."

"Not even studio space?"

"None outside of the basement workspace she keeps at her parents' house. She sells her work at crafts shows, swap meets, flea markets, even at pop—ups, you know, those venues that, literally pop up and then go away as fast as they appeared."

"Kind of like our runaway, huh?"

Carl grinned broadly. Nice analysis, Mattie! Would you like to be my investigative assistant?" He took my hand in his, again squeezing it gently, but not letting go this this time. I felt myself relax for the first time since we boarded the plane, though what lay ahead was anyone's guess.

"I just wish I could have given you something more solid than Peter's letter," I said. "It's only a third-party lead. Elfie never mentioned Key West when she showed up at Ig—Loo. You know the rest..."

"And you never saw her after that one time..."

"That's right. She walked in with a major attitude, wanting something we didn't have on the menu, comparing Ig—Loo to the Tasty Glacier in Coconut Grove. Bea was especially nice to her, though, softened her right up complimenting her outfit. I can't explain why, Carl, but that gal's style, her demeanor, the whole package you could say, unsettled me, but at the same time, it sucked me right in. Jo and Bea were sucked in, too. I thought if anything, Elfie would come back just to say hello, even if our menu didn't suit her. But I actually considered offering her a job. There was something new and different about her, and I was looking to draw more foot traffic to Ig—Loo, to try out new ideas…but Elfie, I mean, *Sara*, never came back."

Recalling that first and last time I'd met Sara Young gave me goosebumps. She had gotten to me then, and she was under my skin now, but for different reasons. It wasn't about the *Double R* anymore.

Carl shifted in his seat, leaning closer to me. "But she still hung around in Miami. She latched onto Peter and, well, here *we* are…" He settled back in his seat.

We. I liked how that sounded. *We* were aboard a plane to Key West. *We* had no idea how we would pinpoint the location of the two people we were determined to find, with no concrete leads, no contacts on the ground to go to.

"Not even a business card," I said, thinking out loud.   All of it, being on this airplane, looking for a runaway and a man I once believed I'd marry, dropping Ig—Loo on Bea's shoulders and Jo's lap while I went on a wild goose chase with a handsome Brit who actually thought I had something to offer his investigation...all of this was bigger than me. But *we*, Carl and me together, yes, *we* could handle it.   At that moment, I had no doubt. And when we returned to Miami, after he'd go his way and I'd go mine, Carl and I would always be a team.

"What business cards, Mattie? Mine?" Carl asked as he buckled his seatbelt.   We were soon to begin our decent, the attendant was announcing over the speaker.

I took his cue and secured my own seatbelt, hoping I didn't look like a rank amateur.

"No, not your cards, " I said, "It's just that you mentioned that Sara had no business cards, and it got me thinking that maybe I should do a little creative designing myself and get on one of those DYI apps. I could make up some snazzy business cards for Ig—Loo."

I spent the next few minutes concentrating on how not to reveal that I was a first—time air traveler. The last thing I wanted to do was to appear scared in front of Carl. Instead, I talked shop, bending Carl's ear about various colors and fonts would look best for the business cards that Ig—Loo would eventually feature.

"Oh, by the way, Carl, Ig—Loo's competition evidently *doesn't* use business cards! We—Jo and I—were at the Tasty Glacier at different times, and never saw them.

"Well, that would be another 'first' under your belt!" Carl winked. I had no idea what he meant by *another*, but there wasn't time to ask.

The next thing I knew, our aircraft was banking to align with our destination, Key West. The drizzle had stopped, the grey clouds had lifted, and now the lower Keys were spread out below like a picture postcard, all blue and green and golden. I'd never been there before. This was *also* "another first" for yours truly!

Carl whispered in my ear, but I couldn't decipher his words, the noise from the landing gear dropping from its holding bay beneath us was deafening. I felt my hand rise with his. He brought my fingers to his lips, kissing them gently. Then he leaned over and kissed me, fully, as the plane touched down. Some passengers clapped as we slowed to taxi to the gate. Were those claps for our safe landing, or for me? I liked to think it was my heart receiving all the applause for coming out of its hiding place, freed from being under lock and key after the end of Peter and me.

...

Carl had long planned to bring the Key West Police in on our search for leads. He was also new to Key West, he'd explained on the plane, so it would be best to check into with the Key West Police as soon as we landed.

Several officers ran names against activities based on our information, but after an hour long data search, nobody named Peter Dawson had contacted law enforcement looking for a young woman named Sally. No one by the names Sally, Sara Young, or Elfie, had been arrested or listed as missing. No complaints were filed by anyone against anyone with any combination of the names, and nobody named Peter, Sara Young, Sally or Elfie had surfaced on any patient admissions printouts at area hospitals. We'd hit a wall.

One of the officers who tried to help us wouldn't give up. Officer Singer got on the telephone, contacting area banks for to determine if anyone using the names we gave her had opened a safe deposit box account. At first, Carl and I didn't understand why Officer Singer had gone to such lengths to speak with the banks.

"If, as you say, Peter Dawson was coming to Key West to find this young woman, Sara Young, who he claims goes by the name of

Sally and who has stolen a valuable ring from his home, maybe *she* decided to separate herself from the ring *just in case* Peter Dawson caught up with her," Officer Singer reasoned.

That made sense to me, but Carl still wasn't convinced.

"Miss Young isn't carrying any identification, I'm sure of that," Carl countered. "No bank would open a safety deposit box for a new customer without some proof of name and address. Sara Young could be going by two other names as well. No, she'd not end up at the bank."

"Maybe she pawned the ring," I suggested.

Officer Singer raised an eyebrow. "Good point. We have two shops here in town. Can either of you give me a description of the diamond?"

Was the photo I took of my left hand to my cheek, with the beautiful ring on my third finger, still saved on my phone, or had I deleted it? I didn't want Carl watching me scroll through my memories. I stepped away from him and Officer Singer and opened my phone camera. I hadn't looked for that photo in two years, but there it was, never deleted. The selfie I'd taken so long ago. The smile on my face caught on camera as I showed off my beautiful ring, my eyes brimming with tears of happiness. Peter had told me after I'd taken the selfie that, when he put the ring on my finger, my eyes sparkled as brightly as the diamond itself. He was right.

Seeing the memory frozen in time took my breath away. I turned to Carl and Officer Singer.

"This is it, the ring. It's mine. I mean, it *was* mine."

I pointed to the screen as if there was need to confirm that the face and the hand were part of the same person. I turned to Carl. The concern on his face told me that he knew how hard this was for me.

"Why don't you stay here in the station, Mattie? I'll check out the two pawn shops. It won't take long, will it, Officer? " A good, idea,

I thought. But I couldn't get the words out. Was I more of a hindrance than a help? Was the photo of the diamond all that was really needed, not a sidekick looking for an ex fiancé?

"The pawn shops are only a few minutes from here," Officer Singer confirmed, "but I'm going off duty in a few minutes. I can go with you off—the—clock. I just need time to change out of my uniform. And..." Officer Singer turned to me, "Mister Statler and I will need to keep your phone with us, Miss Bryant. We need to show the photo."

I handed Carl my phone. "Just please don't pawn it, Carl, or we'll have two rings missing," I replied jokingly. I needed to break the ice. The last thing I wanted was any mention of why, after over two years, I still kept a photo of myself posed with a ring that didn't mean anything anymore.

"Not to worry. "Officer Singer chuckled, catching my comment was she excused herself to log out and change clothes. My weak attempt at humor had not fooled Carl one bit.

"It's going to be okay," Carl said softly. "We'll find Peter for you, Mattie. I promise." He walked me to a bench by the window.

We sat quietly until Officer Singer reappeared, clad in jeans and a tee. She gave me a thumbs—up and called to Carl. "Let's go!"

Though I knew Carl would be in good hands with Officer Singer, no sooner had they left the station than a sense of dread took over. My chest tightened and my thoughts ran roughshod over my common sense. *What if no leads surfaced at either of the pawn shops? What else can we do? Where else can we go?*

My eyes stung. I couldn't fight back the tears. I let them spill where they may as I fumbled for a paper cup at the water cooler that stood beside the bench. My hands shook as I centered the little cup under the stream of icy water. It had been just over a month since Peter's letter showed up in my snail mail, but the diamond ring had to be missing from his house longer than that. Hadn't he written that he'd kept the details from me when he first surfaced with that phone call? Who knows when Sara Young, the imposter Peter had come to know as Sally, actually stole the ring, or even if she had stolen it? And if she did steal it , who knows if she even took it with her to Key West? Maybe it was still stashed away somewhere in Miami. Maybe all of this was just a very bad dream and I'd wake up and find myself back at Ig—Loo with Jo and Bea instead of sitting here in a police station in Key West, trying to track down a man I didn't even know anymore. *Fat chance, Mattie, this is no dream. This is what happens when you break your engagement. All hell will eventually break loose....*

How I missed Bea and Jo! I needed to talk to them right away. I felt for my phone in my back pocket. I remembered then that I'd given the phone to Carl. I scolded myself for being so quick to put myself in a fix, for prioritizing Peter's dilemma over mine. But who had started all of this? I didn't know anymore. My heart raced as it hit me that, aside of Carl and Officer Singer, there was absolutely nobody in this beautiful island city who knew who I was, why I was in Key West, and where I was going next. Shoot, even *yours truly* didn't know the answer to where I'd be this time tomorrow! I was in limbo, scared silly. I must look like hell, too, I thought, as I fished with my free hand through my purse and pockets for something to wipe away the tear streaks that tracked down my cheeks to my chin. *Nothing. No phone, no tissues...brilliant, Mattie.* Instead of drinking my water, I poured some into the palms of my hands and rubbed my face. That's when I heard her.

A rush of movement spilled out from beyond the lobby as three uniformed officers deftly escorted a young woman through a corridor marked Booking. Her high—pitched, sing—song whine echoed from within circle of officers surrounding her.

"I want a lawyer! You have no right to keep

me here!"

I craned my neck to get a better look at the commotion going on in the corridor. But even before I saw her, I'd heard her voice and I knew.

Elfie!

Chapter 12

"Mathilde! Mathilde!"

Peter rushed past Elfie and the police escorts. His voice was unmistakable, but *good grief!* He looked like something out of Elfie's wardrobe closet!

Was this really the man I almost waited a lifetime to marry? I could feel my insides cinch. *Don't get near me, Peter Dawson, or whoever you are these days!*

Peter's once thick head of dark curly hair was dyed neon blue, his ear lobes dripping hoops and bangles, the beginnings of a goatee spouting beneath his lower lip. He was, for lack of a better comparison, an Elfie wannabee, without the elf.

His *Key West Rocks* tee shirt was ripped, mini safety pins closing the slashed fabric, his chest—was that *glitter* on Peter's chest hair?—peeked out from the unpinned places on his tee. His flip flops—was that glitter, too?—

jingled on his feet. *Musical shoes?* I sneaked a closer look. No! Musical *toe rings*!

"Officers! This man...! "I called out to the group of police escorts surrounding Elfie.

I couldn't take my eyes off of Peter. Part of me feared him, but part of me was hypnotized by his metamorphosis. I recoiled against the back of the wooden bench.

One escort broke from the group and pulled up beside Peter. She gave him a withering look as she crooked her finger in his face, signaling him to get back where he was supposed to be going which, I surmised, was most likely to take a mug shot. Why else would he be here? He must have done something, besides dressing crazily.

Peter flinched at the officer's gesture and gave in to her orders. As he backtracked under her watchful eye, he suddenly stopped and did an about face. Our eyes met for a split second.

"*Mister* Dawson," the officer spoke up and placed her hand around his arm, turning him to face her. As he resisted, pulling himself against the strength of her grasp, he yelled, thrashing his arms wildly. More jingles rang out. Peter was a one-man band, an Elfie déjà vu, only with the XY chromosome.

"You wait, Sally! You just wait until I get my hands on you! You are finished!"

"Settle down or I'll have to cuff you, Mister Dawson," the officer warned as she succeeded in positioning him toward the corridor with her free arm, winning the tug of war Peter had started. I watched him fold into himself, rounding his shoulders, shuffling. He muttered something to the officer. She stopped and turned to me.

"Ma'am, are you here about this individual? He says he knows you."

I'd wanted to talk to Peter like I wanted to be back at Ig—Loo, which, trust me, was desperately. But *this* Peter? I shook my head no. *I don't know you, Peter. Not today. Maybe I never did know you...*

"Wait for me, Mathilde, there's something I need from you! Mathilde, you must do...."

Peter's plea faded as he hollered as the officer led him away.

Again, Peter had called me *Mathilde*, as he always had, when he wanted his way.

He always went after my underbelly, always appealing to my willingness to be patient with him, to compromise with him. What did this man need from me now? What must I do now?

During a particularly frustrating time with Peter, I had confided to Aunt Loo. She told me what kept her and Uncle Ig together for such a long time, recalling the good times and bad that she and my uncle had shared, and how they overcame so many twists and turns along the way.

As I tried to recapture the details of my aunt's story, a woman walked into the police station, her hands full with a sobbing child, his chubby fingers wrapped around a candy bar.

"We'll find your family, honey, don't cry," the woman cooed as she tried her best to calm the little boy.

From my spot on the bench, I could hear her explaining to the intake officer how the child had approached her on the street, crying to her that he that he couldn't find his brother and his mother.

"I raised five children," the woman volunteered. "I couldn't leave this child on the street. He didn't want me to bring him here, but I had to do what was best under the circumstances. If I knew where he lived, I'd have taken him home myself, but..."

Aunt Loo's words came back to me then. *When you are in love, you want that person. When you love, you want what's best for that person.*

"We will do our best to locate his family," the intake officer assured the concerned woman. The officer peered down from the high desk and smiled.

"We'll find your mommy. I promise. What's your name, sweetie?"

While the duty officer placed a call, I got up

from the bench. I prepared two cups of water from the cooler and took the cups to the woman. She smiled through worried eyes and offered one of the cups to the little boy. The child drank quickly.

"I'm done." he said, holding up his empty paper cup for me to see.

"Can you find my mommy?" he asked. His dark eyes expressed only trust and hope. "Can you, please?"

Before I could react, a frantic youngster raced into the station.

"Where's Armando? I lost my brother!"

The little boy turned, dropping his candy and the empty paper cup as he ran to the tall boy who shouted his name.

"Dino! I'm here! I'm here!" Armando wrapped his arms about his brother and pointed to the woman who had brought him into the station. "She found me!"

The woman beamed, releasing an audible sigh of relief.

Such a happy reunion, the brothers hugging

each other, their mother on their heels, her face a combination of fear and joy at finding her son safe and in good hands. The family gathered before the duty officer's desk, the boys' mother pulled out some identification for the officer and was cleared to take her brood home. The woman who had brought Armando to the station motioned me to join them.

"I am Dolores," she said. "Thank you for the water."

"Pleased to meet you, Dolores, I'm Mathilde."

She nodded. "Are you plain clothes?"

At first, I wasn't sure what she meant, then realized the obvious: Who, besides uniformed police, or civilians in trouble, hangs out on benches at police stations and passes out cups of water without being asked?

I chuckled. "Oh no, I'm just waiting for a friend. He's trying hard to find someone, too. Small world, huh?"

"I hope everything will work out for your friend, Mathilde," Dolores said, extending her hand.

"Me, too, thank you, Dolores," I replied, returning the gesture. Our handshake expanded to a warm hug before parting ways.

I watched Dolores walk across the street and disappear around the corner, just as I'd watched Carl and Officer Singer do earlier. This time, though, I didn't feel left alone. I also didn't regret having given someone I hadn't known until an hour ago, my real name.

Our little gathering, our group of would—be strangers, who had formed a link in the best interests of a little boy, left me buoyant. I sent up a prayer of thanks that Peter would be okay. For better or for worse, he was being looked after down the corridor, and wasn't going anywhere for now. Where ever he ended up, I knew for certain now that it would be without yours truly by his side. Aunt Loo's words never made more sense, were never so clear in my head and in my heart, as they were right now. *When you love someone...you want what's best for them...*

The best thing that could happen for Carl was to find Sara Young for her family. That's what I wanted. I knew where she was. When Carl and Officer Singer returned, they would learn that Sara and Peter were right here at the station. Where ever this news took Carl, I would be there for him if he wanted me to stay by him.

I wouldn't change my mind and ask the duty officer to take me to Peter. I'd said good—bye visibly, tangibly, long ago, when I took that diamond off my finger. But it wasn't enough to end us.

You have to say goodbye from the inside, Mattie.

I sent up another prayer, this time with thanks for not having been needed out on the streets of Key West.

Chapter 13

"Do you really want to know?"

Carl and I sipped smoothies as we walked the beach at sunset.

"Yes, I really want to know."

Carl draped his arm around my shoulder and pulled me closer to him.

"I think *Mathilde* is a beautiful name. It's rather popular on the other side of the pond." He chuckled. "A chap I know in London married a lady named Grace."

"What does Grace have to do with *my* name?"

Carl's eyes were twinkling. He winked at me and squeezed my shoulder. "Grace's poodle is named Mathilde."

"Oh stop that!" I punched Carl's arm playfully.

The wind was picking up. And we had a plane to catch later tonight.

"I hope we have a smooth flight," Carl said.

"I don't like flying, you know."

"You could have fooled me!" I said, remembering how calm he was this morning when our plane flew into turbulence.

We had no luggage, which was a blessing Carl said, because it was less to carry or remember. Our twelve hours in Key West had been frantic. We'd gone on a day long, do or die search for clues to the whereabouts of two people, following leads from a phone call and a letter from one of them, coming up empty, even with the help from a kindly off—duty police officer. I'd not forget Officer Singer any time soon, and made a mental note to have a gallon of Ig—Loo's Rum Runner Raison packed in dry ice and shipped express—rush to the station with her name on it.

All I wanted now was to decompress. I didn't want to rehash what had happened at the station when Carl and Officer Singer returned from checking out the pawn shops. It was still a blur, and I have to admit I preferred keeping it that way.

I remembered only a few things: Officer Singer trying to hand back my phone, apologizing for coming up empty, while yours truly hollered, *They're here! They're here!* I remembered Officer Singer trying again: *Yes, we're back, please take your phone,* and yours truly shouting to Carl and pointing to the corridor*: Sara Young! Peter Dawson! They're here!*

I remember Officer Singer grabbing my hand, closing my fingers over my phone before breaking into a run toward the corridor, and Carl, his fists clenched, then opening, pulling me close.

•••

Carl said he was fine forgetting the events of the day for a couple of hours before we had to fly back to Miami. He had contacted Sara's parents, and while he hated to confirm that Sara was under arrest, was relieved when Mr.

and Mrs. Young told him that Sara used her one phone call privilege to call home.

"Sara's folks are flying down first thing tomorrow. My work is done, but theirs is just beginning."

"So is Peter's," I said.

Who knew what would happen to Peter? That he needed help was obvious. But help wouldn't come, *couldn't* come, from yours truly, whether I was Mattie or Mathilde, to him. I knew that now.

We had been dead wrong for each other from the start. No wonder no wedding date ever stuck. No wonder even a gorgeous diamond ring couldn't seal the deal.

Being *in* love was the easy part. Loving took work. Neither Peter nor I had wanted to work that hard for each other. Still, when Peter's letter had arrived in my mailbox, I'd almost...almost...

Carl nudged my arm. "So, tell me why you don't like your real name. I'm very curious."

I broke from Carl to examine a seashell

washed up upon the soft sand. As I was looking for seashells, Carl was looking for answers.

"On the plane home, I promise, I'll tell you." I said. I dropped to one knee to pick up the shell.

"It's that bad, huh?" Carl asked softly. "Sorry for being so bloody pushy."

I counted the ridges on the shell's surface. *Best that you concentrate on something, Mattie.* If I got into the weeds with Carl about my name, I'd be telling him something I didn't want just anybody to know.

But this man isn't just anybody. My stomach flipped just like it had when we were in the air.

I sucked up the last of my smoothie.

"This was *delish!* Maybe Ig—Loo should feature smoothies along with all those new flavors..."

I handed Carl my empty cup. "Would you mind rinsing this in the tide? I could use it to hold the shells."

Carl placed my cup, and his own, on the

sand. He took me in his arms and pulled me to his chest.

"*You're* delish," he whispered, then kissed me, long and deeply. My little seashell fell from my hand, landing in the soft sand where it belonged. Carl followed it, taking me with him.

The plane...we'll miss it...

Shhh, listen. Feel us.

My hand over his heart, his breath in my hair.

We're already flying...

Chapter 14

"I know it's silly that I had such thin skin about my name. I always thought it was a stuffy, old-fashioned name. And Peter knew I hated being called..."

I stopped myself. "Sorry. Come lay your head down. You have a long flight ahead."

"Hmmm, I love your lap, so soft...."

"I could stand to lose some weight, you know!"

"You're perfect—o. Don't change a thing except your *last* name this time next spring."

We finished our coffee. I'd put a spoonful of Rum Runner Raisin in each mug. Aunt Loo told me how delicious a morning coffee tasted with a dollop of Ig—Loo's best—selling flavor floated on top. Better than whipped cream, she'd promised.

"How did you like it?"

Carl wrinkled his nose. "I'm not sure yet. I have to try it more than once. Did your aunt give this concoction a name?

"Gee, I don't know. Let's call it faux spiked Colombian roast." I took our empty mugs into the kitchen then returned to Carl's arms.

"Carl, do you remember in Key West, on the beach, when you kept asking me why I didn't like my name? I told you I'd let you know when we were on the plane, but we missed the plane..."

"How could I *not* remember? While we waited for a later flight, I asked you to marry me." He winked. "And you said you weren't sure."

"I needed you to ask more than once," I joked.

Carl rolled his eyes. "Okay, okay, I get it. Very well then, I've decided I don't need to try your aunt's invention more than once. I *love* the Rum Runner Raisin with coffee. And I don't care what name it goes by. How's *that*, my soon to be Mrs. *Mathilde* Statler?"

Coming from Carl, my given name is golden, literally. For years I'd endured cruel comments from classmates. The two that especially stuck were *Hey, Mathilde, are you named after Waltzing Matilda?* and, *That's an Old Maid's name!* Later, Peter played his head games, always using *Mathilde* when he wanted to lecture, correct, patronize, or insult me.

When I opened up to Carl about how I'd felt all those years, he gave me a necklace of the finest 24 carat gold, with *Mathilde* embossed in beautifully flowing script on a heart—shaped pendant. On the back of the pendant, the ultimate compliment: *What's In a Name? Everything You!*

I stroked the beautiful pendant—I wore it twenty—four—seven—and drew Carl close for one last time. His mustache, still wet from the ice cream and coffee, tickled my cheek. He stretched and pulled himself up from the couch.

"I bloody wish I didn't have to go," he groaned.

"I know, but it's best for you, Carl. You need to close your office in Gainesville, and you must spend some time back home. You haven't seen your family for a long time."

We slow danced in the living room before he left. We didn't turn on any music though. Rather, we just danced to the beat of our hearts. *We'll still be liked this when we get old, and our kids will laugh and ask what's wrong, swaying like that, holding on to each other so tightly. We'll bring the kids to us and invite them to sway with us. We'll make our own music.*

"Send me real letters sometimes, while I'm overseas, could you, Mathilde? Something I can show my parents. They don't do digital. They're old school. Am *I* sounding too old school? I just want something I can hold, to keep close, surrounded by your fragrance."

"Carl, you know I don't ever wear perfume."

"You don't have to. *You are* my perfume."

Epilogue

Dearest Carl,

I promised Aunt Loo that I'd relay a message with my first handwritten letter. Brace for impact: Aunt Loo says to tell you she is extremely upset that you closed Statler Investigations to go into ice cream, managing Ig—Loo with me. She says you are "a man of intrigue" who needs more danger and excitement than Ig—Loo can offer. Uncle Ig says that he is a man of intrigue, too, even though he doesn't know what that means when it comes to his own personal definition of danger and excitement. Aunt Loo ordered him not to go there! Those two are a bloody riot! Seriously, though, my aunt and uncle are thrilled that we're getting married. They send all their love, and promise to return from the road for our wedding. And speaking of weddings…

The talk around town is that Peter Dawson

and Sara Young got engaged! Bea is taking bets on whether Peter gave Sara the same diamond he swears she stole from him. What a pair. They are so totally meant for each other!

I just hope they don't show up in Miami and try to crash our ice—cream and cocktails ferryboat reception on Biscayne Bay....though, if they did, what do you say we let them stay? After all, if "Elfie" hadn't come to Ig—Loo on a quest for the Double R....you and I may still be looking for each other!

Speaking of diamonds...since you asked, let's not. The necklace says it all. That is my "engagement" ring. We can exchange simple bands of gold on our wedding day. What we've got already says more than a diamond ever could.

Jo and Bea send their best! Hurry back, my wonderful you. I want another rendezvous.

Love,

Mathilde

Acknowledgements

To the editors at Blossom Spring Publishing, and to Claire Voet, Publishing Manager, for taking an interest in working with me to bring this book to life. I am deeply grateful for your guidance and support.

To those friends and colleagues from the Philadelphia Writers' Conference, your enthusiasm for my many projects over the years continues to inspire and excite. Thank you, one and all.

Follow Author Harriet G. Fry on Angelfire and LinkedIn

https://bookmarkavenue.angelfire.com/

https://www.linkedin.com/in/harriet—g— fry—16667358/

www.blossomspringpublishing.com

www.ingramcontent.com/pod-product-compliance
Lightning Source LLC
Chambersburg PA
CBHW030306130626
46549CB00002B/729